Ena put her hand on his chest. Warmth instantly generated from the points of contact. "What if I told you that I'm not afraid?"

"I'd tell you that you should be." He said the words so quietly they sounded more like an invitation than a reason for her to flee.

"Let me be the judge of that," she told him, her lips so close to his now that he could almost taste the words as she uttered them.

And that finally did it. Mitch lost what little control he was trying so desperately to hang on to.

The next second, he was no longer attempting to block his urges. Instead, he pulled Ena to him, his arms wrapping around her as he lowered his mouth to hers.

And then he did what he'd been wanting to do since the very first moment he had laid eyes on her back in high school more than ten years ago.

He kissed her.

* * *

FOREVER, TEXAS:
Cowboys, ranchers and lawmen—oh my!

Dear Reader,

Ena O'Rourke couldn't wait to leave Forever. She and her father never got along, and after her mother died, it just became worse. So bad that the day after she graduated from high school, she took off, relocating to Dallas and reinventing herself. She is now a successful accountant in a major firm. A letter from her father's attorney brings her back to Forever and the family ranch. According to the terms of her father's will, if she wants to inherit the ranch, she needs to work on it for six months. Ena is furious, but she isn't about to walk away because that would prove her father right. She is a quitter.

Mitch Parnell lost both of his parents while still in his teens. He was an outcast until Ena's father took him under his wing the same day that Ena took off for Dallas. Loyal to a fault and secretly in love with Ena since he first saw her in high school, Mitch is determined to make her see that her father wasn't the dark ogre she thought he was. He is there to help her through the various hurdles and also to convince her that she shouldn't sell the ranch. The path is not smooth by any means, but it is one he feels she will always regret if she winds up turning her back on it.

I hope I've aroused your curiosity just a little. If so, I thank you for taking the time to read one of my books, and from the bottom of my heart, I wish you someone to love who loves you back.

All the best,

Marie Ferrarella

Her Right-Hand Cowboy

Marie Ferrarella

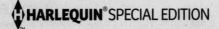
HARLEQUIN® SPECIAL EDITION

Recycling programs
for this product may
not exist in your area.

ISBN-13: 978-1-335-89429-8

Her Right-Hand Cowboy

Copyright © 2019 by Marie Rydzynski-Ferrarella

Printed in U.S.A.

www.Harlequin.com

USA TODAY bestselling and RITA® Award—winning author **Marie Ferrarella** has written more than two hundred and fifty books for Harlequin, some under the name Marie Nicole. Her romances are beloved by fans worldwide. Visit her website, marieferrarella.com.

Books by Marie Ferrarella

Harlequin Special Edition

Matchmaking Mamas

Coming Home for Christmas
Dr. Forget-Me-Not
Twice a Hero, Always Her Man
Meant to Be Mine
A Second Chance for the Single Dad
Christmastime Courtship
Engagement for Two
Adding Up to Family
Bridesmaid for Hire

Forever, Texas

The Cowboy's Lesson in Love
The Lawman's Romance Lesson

The Fortunes of Texas: The Lost Fortunes

Texan Seeks Fortune

The Fortunes of Texas: The Secret Fortunes

Fortune's Second-Chance Cowboy

***The Montana Mavericks:
The Great Family Roundup***

The Maverick's Return

Visit the Author Profile page
at Harlequin.com for more titles.

To
Charlie,
My one and only
Love,
After fifty-one years together,
You still make the world fade away
Every time you kiss me.

Chapter One

It felt familiar, yet strange.

The closer she came to the sprawling two-story ranch house, the simple five-word sentence kept repeating itself over and over again in Ena O'Rourke's brain like a tuneless song. Part of her just couldn't believe that she had returned here after all this time.

She could remember when she couldn't wait to get away from here. Or rather not "here" but away from her father because, to her then eighteen-year-old mind, Bruce O'Rourke was the source of all the anger and pain that existed in her world. Back then, she and her father were constantly at odds and without Edith, her mother, to act as a buffer, Ena and her father were forever butting heads.

The way she saw it, her father was opinionated, and he never gave her any credit for being right, not even once. After enduring a state of what felt like constant warfare for two years, ever since her mother lost her battle with cancer, Ena made up her mind and left the ranch, and Forever, one day after high school graduation.

At the time, she had been certain that she would never come back, had even sworn to herself that she wouldn't. And although she wavered a little in the first couple of years or so, as she struggled to put herself through college, she had stuck by her promise and kept far away from the source of all her unhappiness.

Until now.

She swung her long legs out of her light blue sports car and got out. She had sincerely doubted that a man who had always seemed to be bigger than life itself was ever going to die.

Until he did.

Bruce O'Rourke had died as tight-lipped as he had lived, without ever having uttered a single word to her. He had never even tried to get in contact with her. It was as if, for him, she had never existed.

It figured, Ena thought now, slowly approaching the house where she had grown up. Her father hadn't bothered to get in contact with her to tell her that he was dying. Instead, he had his lawyer summon her the moment he was gone. That way, he hadn't given her a chance to clear the air or vent her feelings.

He hadn't wanted to be held accountable.

Because he knew he had driven her away, she thought now, angry tears gathering in her eyes.

"Same old Dad," she bit off angrily.

She remained where she was for a moment, just staring at the exterior of the old ranch house. She had expected to see it on the verge of falling apart. But apparently her father had been careful not to allow that to happen. He had taken care of the homestead. The house looked as if it was sporting a brand-new coat of paint that couldn't have been more than a few months old.

She frowned to herself. Bruce O'Rourke took a great deal more care of the house and the ranch than he ever had when dealing with her. Her mother, Ena recalled with a stab of pain, was the only one who could effectively deal with the man. What Edith had advised her on more than one occasion was to just give the man a pass because he was under so much pressure and had so much responsibility on his shoulders. It wasn't easy, the genteel woman had told her in that soft low-key voice of hers, trying to keep the ranch going.

"So you kept it going while pushing me away—and what did it get you in the end, Old Man? You're gone, and the ranch is still here. At least for now," she said ironically. "But not for long. Just until I can get someone to take it off my hands. And then I'll finally be done with it, and you, once and for all," Ena concluded under her breath.

She was stalling. She supposed she was putting off dealing with that oppressive wave of memories that threatened to wash over her the moment she walked through the front door and into the house.

But she knew that she couldn't put it off indefinitely.

Taking a deep breath, she squared her shoulders and took another tentative step toward the house. And then another until she reached the steps leading up to the wraparound veranda. The place, she recalled, where her mother and father used to like to sit and rock at the end of the day.

As she came to the second step, Ena heard that old familiar creak beneath her foot.

Her father never had gotten around to fixing that. She

could remember her mother asking him to see to it and her father promising to *"get to it when I have the time."*

"Obviously you never found the time to fix that that, either, did you, Old Man?" she said, addressing the man who was no longer there.

"Is that a Dallas thing? Talking to yourself?" a deep male voice behind her asked.

In the half second that it took Ena to swing around to see who had crept up so silently behind her, she managed to compose herself and not look as if the tall, handsome, dark-haired cowboy behind her had launched her heart into double time.

"Is sneaking up behind people something you picked up while working here?" Ena countered, annoyed.

Her father had had that habit, materializing behind her when she least expected it, usually to interrogate her about where she had been or where she intended on going. And no matter what she answered, her father always sounded as if he disapproved and was criticizing her.

The cowboy, however, sounded contrite. "Sorry, I didn't realize I wasn't making enough noise for you." He then coughed and cleared his throat. "Is that loud enough?" he asked her with an easy grin.

Ena pressed her lips together and glared at him without answering.

The cowboy nodded. "I take it from that look on your face that you don't remember me," he said.

Ena narrowed her clear blue eyes as she focused on the cowboy, who must have towered over her by at least a good twelve inches. There was something vaguely familiar about his rugged face with its high, almost gaunt cheekbones, but after the restless night she had spent and then the long trip back, she was *not* in the mood to play guessing games with someone who was apparently one of her father's ranch hands.

"Should I?" she asked coldly.

Mitch Parnell winced. "Ouch, I guess that puts me in my place," he acknowledged. He pushed back his worn Stetson and took off his right glove, extending his hand out to her. "Welcome home, Ena."

The deep smile and familiar tone nudged forward more memories from her past. Her eyes slowly swept over the dusty, rangy cowboy. It couldn't be—

Could it?

"Mitch?" she asked uncertainly. But even as she said his name, part of her thought she was making a mistake.

Until he smiled.

Really smiled.

Even as a teenager, Mitch Parnell had always had the kind of smile that the moment it appeared, it could completely light up the area. She and Mitch had gone to high school together, and for a week or two, she had even fancied herself in love with him—or as in love as a seventeen-year-old unhappy, lost girl desperately searching for acceptance could be.

Her mother had died the year before and communication between her father and her had gone from bad to worse. It felt as if the only times Bruce O'Rourke spoke to her, he was either lashing out at her or yelling at her. Hurting, she had been desperate to find a small haven, some sort of a retreat from the cold world where she could pretend she was loved and cared for.

But at seventeen, she had been awkward and not exactly skilled in womanly wiles. Consequently, she just assumed that Mitch had missed all her signals. It even felt as if he had dodged all her outright romantic gestures. In any event, she wound up withdrawing even further into herself, biding her time until she finally graduated high school and could flee the site of her unhappiness.

At the time, Mitch had just been someone she'd gone to school with. If anything, he had been a further reminder of her failure to make a connection with someone. She didn't associate him with her father's ranch. Had he come to work here after he had graduated high school? The few conversations they'd had back then, he had never mentioned anything about wanting to work on a ranch. Seeing him here was a surprise.

It occurred to her that she knew next to nothing about the good-looking guy she had briefly thought of as her salvation.

"Mitch?" she repeated, still looking at him, confused.

Pleasure brought an even wider smile to his lips. "So you do remember me." There was satisfaction evident in his voice.

Ena fervently hoped that he merely thought of her as someone he'd gone to school with and not as the girl who had made an unsuccessful play for him. This was already awkward enough as it was.

"What are you doing here?" she asked.

"I work here," Mitch answered. His tone was neither boastful nor solicitous. He was merely stating a fact. "As a matter of fact, your dad made me foreman of the Double E almost three years ago."

Ena stared at him, trying to comprehend what Mitch was telling her. When she'd left, her father only hired men to work on the ranch who he'd either known for years or who came highly recommended by men he had known for years. Apparently, some things had changed in the last ten years.

"Where's Rusty?" she asked, referring to the big barrel-chested man who had been her father's foreman for as long as she could remember.

The smile on Mitch's lips faded, giving way to a somber expression. "Rusty died."

She stared at Mitch in disbelief. "When?" she finally asked.

This was almost more than she could process. Rusty Hayes had been the man who had taught her how to ride a horse. When she was really young, she remembered wishing that Rusty was her real father and not the man who periodically growled at her and even growled at her mother on occasion. Rusty had been even-tempered. Her father couldn't have been accused of that.

"Three years ago," Mitch told her. There was sympathy in his eyes. "You didn't know," he guessed.

"There's a lot I didn't know," Ena bit off. "My father and I didn't exactly stay in touch," she added angrily, trying to process this latest blow.

Mitch continued to look at her sympathetically. "So I gather." She was still standing on the top step of the veranda. He decided that maybe she needed a gentle nudge. "Would you like to go in?" he asked.

The question seemed to snap her out of the deep funk she had slipped into. Ena pulled her shoulders back as if she were gearing up for battle. "I lived here for eighteen years. I don't need your invitation to go in if that's what I want to do," she informed him.

Mitch raised his hands up in mute surrender. "Didn't mean to imply that you did," he told her, apologizing without saying the actual words. The next moment, he saw her turning on her heel. She walked down the three steps, away from the porch. "Are you leaving?" he asked her in surprise.

"Are you trying to keep tabs on me?" she demanded.

To Ena's surprise, rather than answer her, Mitch began to laugh. Heartily.

Scowling, she snapped, "I wasn't aware that I had said something funny."

It took him a second to catch his breath. "Not exactly funny," he told her.

Her eyes had narrowed to small slits that were all but shooting daggers at him. "Then what?" she asked.

This whole situation had made her decidedly uncomfortable, as well as angry. This person she had gone to school with—and had briefly entertained feelings for—was acting more at ease and at home on this property than she was. For some reason, that irritated her to no end.

Mitch took in another deep breath so he could speak. "I was just thinking how much you sounded like your father."

If he had intentionally tried to set her off, he couldn't have found a better way. Anger creased Ena's forehead.

Struggling not to lose her temper, she informed him, "I am *nothing* like my father."

Mitch's response was to stare at her as if he were trying to discern whether or not she was kidding him. Before he could stop himself, he asked in amazement, "You honestly believe that?"

"Yes," Ena ground out between clenched teeth, "I honestly do."

The smile on Mitch's face was almost radiant. He pressed his lips together to keep from laughing again, sensing that she really wouldn't appreciate it if he did. But he couldn't refrain from saying, "Wow, you really *are* like your father."

No wonder her father had made this man his foreman. Mitch Parnell was as crazy in his own way as her father had been. "Stop saying that," she insisted.

"Okay," he agreed good-naturedly, relenting. "But it doesn't make it any less true."

Ena curled her fingers into her palms. She wasn't going to give Mitch a piece of her mind, even though she would have liked nothing better than to tell him what an infuriating idiot he was. Which only left her with one option.

Ena turned on her heel and headed back to her vehicle—quickly.

Mitch followed at a pace that others might refer to as walking briskly, but he cut the distance between them so effortlessly it didn't even look as if he was walking fast.

"Hey, was it something I said?" he asked. "If it helps, I can apologize," he said, although he had no idea what he could have said to set her off.

But because he had just lost a boss who over the years had become more like a surrogate father to him, Mitch was willing to apologize to Bruce's daughter. He knew that having her here would have meant a lot to his boss. Besides, he had looked into Ena's eyes, and while she probably thought she had covered up things well, he had glimpsed pain there. Having her run off like this wasn't going to eliminate that pain.

"I came to see the ranch house," Ena informed him crisply. "And I saw it. Now I'm going to see my father's lawyer and find out what he has to tell me so I know exactly where I stand."

"You're talking about your dad's will." It wasn't a guess on Mitch's part.

Ena's antenna went up. The accounting firm in Dallas where she had worked her way up to a junior partnership had seen all manner of fraud. Fraud that had been the result of greed and a sense of entitlement. Initially, when she had first encountered it, she had been surprised by the way people treated one another when a little bit of money was involved. But eventually, she came to expect it, just as she now expected to have to fight Mitch on some level because he had probably come to regard the ranch as his own and had hung around, waiting for her father to die. He undoubtedly expected to have her father leave the ranch to him.

Maybe, for all she knew, Mitch had even helped the situation along.

Well, too bad, she thought. If her father *had* left the ranch to his "trusty foreman," Mitch Parnell was going to have one hell of a fight on his hands.

Calm down, Ena. You're jumping the gun and getting way ahead of yourself, she silently counseled.

But she wasn't here to try to prove that Mitch had somehow brought about her father's demise because he had designs on the Double E. She was here to try to make the best of the situation, sell the ranch and move on. With any luck, by the end of the week she could put her whole childhood behind her once and for all.

Starting up her car, she half expected Mitch to run up to her window and try to stop her—or to at least say something inane such as "Don't do anything hasty." But as she pulled away, the foreman remained standing just where he was.

She could see him in the rearview mirror, watching her and shaking his head.

The smug bastard. Was he judging her?

Deep breaths, Ena, she instructed herself. *Deep breaths. You can't let someone out of your past get to you. You're here to listen to the reading of the will and to sell the ranch. The sooner you do that, the sooner things will get back to being normal and you can go on with your life.*

A life she had fought hard to forge, she reminded herself. On her own. Without asking for so much as a single dime from her father.

She was proud of that.

At the same time, the fact that she had had to do it on her own, without any help, or even an offer of help, from her father managed to sting bitterly. It reinforced her feelings of being by herself. She hadn't always been alone. There'd been another child, her twin brother, but the baby had died at birth. While her mother had treated her as if she were a perpetual special gift from Heaven, she had always felt that her father resented that she had been the one to live and her brother had been the one to die.

"Sorry, Old Man," she caught herself saying as she drove into town, on the lookout for the attorney's office—there had been no lawyers in Forever when she had left. "Those were the cards you were dealt. You should have made the most of it. I would have made you forget all about the son you never had. But you never gave me the chance." She shrugged, her shoulders rising and then falling again carelessly. "Your loss," she concluded.

The next moment, not wanting to put up with the silence within her car a second longer, Ena turned on the radio and let Johnny Cash mute her pain.

Chapter Two

Mitch watched as Ena's rather impressive but highly impractical car—at least for this part of the country—become smaller and smaller until it was barely a moving dot on the winding road.

She had come back, he marveled. He'd had his doubts there for a minute or two after Bruce O'Rourke had died and Cash, her father's lawyer, had sent a letter to notify Ena, but she had come back.

Ena was even more beautiful than he'd remembered, Mitch thought. Hell, every memory involving her was sealed away in his mind, including the very first time he ever laid eyes on her.

He smiled to himself now, recalling the event as if it were yesterday. It was a Tuesday. Second period English class. He'd been a new transfer to the high school and had just been handed his class schedule. He'd walked into Mrs. Brickman's class fifteen minutes after it had officially started.

Everyone's eyes in the class had been focused on "the new kid" as he walked in the door, doing his damnedest to look as if he didn't care what anyone thought of him, even though he did.

And then, as his eyes quickly swept over the small class, he saw *her*. Ena O'Rourke. Blue eyes and long blond hair. Sitting up front, second seat, fourth row. He caught himself thinking that she was the most beautiful girl who had ever walked the face of the earth.

He'd almost swallowed his tongue.

It took everything he had to continue with his blasé act, appearing as if he didn't care one way or another about any of these people.

But he did. He cared what they all thought.

Especially the blonde little number in front.

And because she had suddenly become so very important to him, he deliberately acted as if he didn't give a damn what any of these people thought of him. Especially her.

With a Navajo mother and an Irish father, Mitch felt as if he had one foot in each world and yet belonged nowhere.

He remembered Ena smiling at him. Remembered Mrs. Brickman telling him to take the empty seat next to *Miss O'Rourke*.

Remembered his stomach squeezing so hard he could hardly breathe.

Wanting desperately to come across as his own person and not some pitiful newcomer, he had maintained an aloof aura and deliberately kept everyone at arm's length, even the girl who reduced his knees to the consistency of melted butter.

Why had he ever been that young and stupid? he now

wondered. But life, back then, for an outsider hadn't been easy.

It hadn't become easier, he recalled, until Bruce O'Rourke had gruffly given him a chance and hired him to work the ranch shortly after his parents died, leaving him an orphan.

Funny the turns that life took, he mused.

Mitch observed Wade McCallister making his way over to him. The heavyset older man looked more than a little curious. He jerked a thumb at the departing vehicle. "Hey, boss, was that—"

Mitch didn't wait for the other man to finish his question. He already knew what the ranch hand was going to ask and nodded his head.

"Yup, it was."

Wade had worked off and on at the Double E Ranch for a long time. Long enough to have known Bruce O'Rourke's daughter before she was even a teenager.

Turning now to watch Ena's car become less than a speck on the horizon, Wade asked, "Where's she heading off to?"

"She's on her way to talk to the old man's lawyer," Mitch answered. Even the dot he'd been watching was gone now. He turned away from the road and focused his attention on Wade.

Wade's high forehead was deeply furrowed. The ranch hand had never been blessed with a poker face. "She's gonna sell the ranch, isn't she?" the older man asked apprehensively.

"She might want to," Mitch answered. "But she can't." His smile grew deeper. "At least not yet."

"What do you mean she can't?" Wade asked him, confused.

Wade had known Bruce O'Rourke longer than Mitch

had. But Wade didn't have a competitive bone in his body and he wasn't insulted that his normally close-mouthed boss had taken Mitch into his confidence. As a result, Mitch had been devoted to the old man and everyone knew it. While the rest of them had lives of their own apart from the ranch, Mitch had made himself available to Bruce 24/7, ready to run errands for him no matter what time of day or night. No job was too great or too small as far as Mitch was concerned.

"The old man put that in his will." He had been one of Bruce O'Rourke's two witnesses when his boss had had the will drawn up and then had him sign it. Afterward, Bruce had expanded on what he had done. "He said the ranch was hers on the sole condition that she stay here and run things for six months."

It sounded good, but it was clear that Wade had his doubts the headstrong girl he'd watched grow up would adhere to the will.

"What if she decides not to listen to that—what do you call it? A clause?" Wade asked, searching for the right term.

Mitch nodded. "A clause," he confirmed. "If she doesn't, then the ranch gets turned over to some charitable foundation Mr. O'Rourke was partial to."

The furrows on Wade's forehead were back with a vengeance. "Does that mean we're all out of a job? 'Cause I'm too old to go looking for work with my hat in my hand."

Mitch shook his head and laughed at the picture the other man was attempting to paint. "Too old? Hell, Wade, you're not even fifty."

Wade wasn't convinced. "I'd have to pull up stakes and try to find some kind of work somewhere else, and

I'm comfortable where I am." The ranch hand's frown deepened. "Like I said, too old."

"Well, don't go packing up your saddlebags just yet," Mitch told the man he regarded as his right-hand man. "Even if the ranch does get sold down the line, whatever organization takes over is doubtlessly going to want the ranch to keep on turning a profit. But don't worry," Mitch assured the other man. "The old man was banking on the idea that once his daughter gets back to her roots, she's not going to want to let this place go."

Wade, however, wasn't convinced—with good reason, he felt. "You weren't here when she left. To be honest, I'm surprised the old man's daughter came back at all."

"Oh, I don't know," Mitch said, thinking back to his own childhood and adolescence. It had taken him time to make peace with who he was and where he had come from. Now he was proud of it, but it hadn't always been that way. "Our past has a greater hold on us than we'd like to believe."

But Wade was still far from swayed. And other problems occurred to him. "Even if she does wind up keeping it, she's bound to make changes in the way the ranch is run."

Mitch was used to Wade's pessimism. It hadn't been all that long ago that he had been just like Wade, seeing the world in shades of black. But then Bruce had taken him under his wing and everything had changed from that day forward.

"Let's not get ahead of ourselves," Mitch advised. "Let's just see how her visit with the old man's lawyer goes."

Wade took in a deep breath, centering himself. "Okay, you're the boss, Mitch."

Mitch grinned. "That's right. I am. At least for now," he allowed, deliberately playing on the other man's natural penchant for gloom and doom.

For Wade's sake, as well as for the sake of all the other men who worked under him at the Double E Ranch, Mitch maintained a positive attitude. The old man had taught him that there was nothing to be gained by wallowing in negative thoughts, saying that he himself had learned that the hard way. If things went well, then being negative was just a waste. And if things didn't go well, there was no point in hurrying things along. They'd catch up to him soon enough.

Besides, who knew? Mitch thought. Maybe coming back here would help heal whatever was broken within Ena's soul.

"C'mon," Mitch urged, turning toward Wade. "We've still got work to do."

Forever had built up since she'd been here last, Ena thought as she drove down the town's long Main Street. The last time she'd been here, the town's medical clinic had been boarded up, the way it had been for close to thirty years. From what she could see by the vehicles jammed in the small parking lot, the clinic was open and doing a healthy business.

She smiled to herself at her unintentional pun.

And that was new, Ena noted as she continued to travel along Forever's Main Street. Slowing her vehicle, she took a closer look at what appeared to be—*a hotel?*

Surprised, she slowed down even more as she passed a small welcoming three-story building. Yes, it was a hotel all right.

Was there actually an influx of tourists to Forever

these days? Enough to warrant building and running a hotel? Was it even profitable?

Ena looked over her shoulder again as she passed the new building. She had never thought that progress would actually ever come to Forever. Obviously she had thought wrong.

The law firm where she was supposed to go to see her father's lawyer was new, as well—as was the concept of her father actually *having* a will formally drafted and written up. If her father had actually *wanted* to put down any final instructions to be followed after his demise, she would have expected him to write them down himself by hand on the inside of some old brown paper grocery bag, its insides most likely stained and making the writing illegible.

To see a lawyer would have taken thought on his part, a process that she had a hard time crediting her father with. Anyway, to draw up a will would have been an admission of mortality, and from the bottom of her heart, she was certain that her father had honestly believed he was going to live forever.

He'd certainly conducted himself that way while she lived here.

Ena realized that she was driving past the diner. She caught herself wondering if that, too, had changed. Was Miss Joan still running the place? She couldn't bring herself to imagine that not being the case. Miss Joan had been a fixture in Forever for as long as she could remember.

When she'd been a young girl, Ena could remember that she'd been afraid of the sharp-tongued woman. It was only as she got older that she began to appreciate the fact that everyone turned to Miss Joan for advice or support, even though, at least on the surface, Miss Joan was a no-nonsense, opinionated, blustery woman who could cut to the heart of any matter faster than anyone she'd ever met.

Ena made a mental note to stop by the diner when she finished with her father's lawyer. She wanted to see for herself if Miss Joan was still running the place.

And, while she was at it, she wanted to ask Miss Joan why *she* at least hadn't gotten in contact with her to tell her that her father was dying of cancer. Never mind that she hadn't given the woman her address or phone number and had maintained her own silence for ten years. Miss Joan had her ways of getting in contact with people. She always had.

After pulling up in front of the neat, hospitable, small freshly painted building with its sign proclaiming Law Offices, Ena carefully parked her sports car.

As she emerged out of the vehicle, she saw a couple of vaguely familiar-looking people passing by. They were looking in her direction as they walked. By the expressions on their faces, they appeared to be trying to place her, as well.

Getting this uncomfortable bit of business over and done with was the only thing on her mind at the moment. She looked away from the duo and went up to the law office's front door.

Ena had barely rung the bell when the door swung open. She found herself making eye contact with a tall, good-looking, blond-haired man she didn't recognize. The man had a friendly, authoritative air about him despite his age, which she judged to be somewhere around his late thirties.

Ena dived right in. "Hello, I have an appointment with Cash Taylor," she told the man.

Warm, friendly eyes crinkled at her as he smiled.

"Yes, I know. I'm Cash—and you're right on time," he told her. "That isn't as usual as you might think." Cash opened the door all the way. "Won't you come in?"

"Thank you," Ena murmured, making her way into the small homey lobby. And then she turned toward Cash, waiting.

"My office is on the right," he told her, sensing his late client's daughter was waiting for him to tell her which direction to go in.

There were two main offices in the building. Cash had one, while the sheriff's wife, who had initially started the firm when she married Sheriff Santiago, had the other. Both were of equal size.

"This is new," Ena heard herself saying as she followed Cash into his tastefully decorated office.

"It is," Cash agreed. "Although I can't take credit for it. My partner started the firm when she decided to stay in Forever after she married Sheriff Santiago."

"Sheriff Rick's married?" Ena asked, surprised by the information.

Cash nodded. "Married and a father. So am I." Not that she probably remembered him, Cash thought. However, there was someone she probably did remember from her early days in Forever. "You might know my wife. She was Alma Rodriguez before she decided to take a chance on me," he told her with an engaging smile.

The surprises just kept on coming, Ena marveled. "You're married to Alma?"

Cash was obviously proud of that fact. He nodded. "You've been gone ten years, is it?" As he sat down at his desk, he checked the notes in the open file before him. "I guess you have a lot of catching up to do."

"I don't plan to stay here long enough to catch up,"

Ena politely informed him. "I'm just here long enough to get the property ready to put up for sale and then I'm going back to Dallas."

Cash frowned slightly. "I'm afraid you're going to have to postpone your return back to Dallas," he informed her politely.

Ena's eyes widened as she stared at the lawyer. "Wait, what? Why?"

Cash realized that he had forgotten one very important step. Extending his hand to her, he said, "First of all, please allow me to express my condolences on the death of your father—" He got no further.

Ena waved her hand, symbolically wiping away whatever else he had to say along those lines. She didn't want his sympathy or anyone else's.

"You can save your breath, Mr. Taylor," Ena said. "My father's been dead to me a long time, just as, I assume, I have been dead to him."

Cash shook his head, wanting to correct her mistaken belief. "I'm afraid I—"

"If he didn't tell you, Mr. Taylor, let me," Ena volunteered. "From the minute I was born, my father and I never got along. After my mother died, that hostility just increased by a factor of ten. I took off the day after I graduated from high school. And I've never looked back." That wasn't strictly true, but she saw no point in elaborating.

Cash nodded. "Yes, your father told me."

Ena shifted in her seat, uncomfortable at the very idea of being here. "To be honest, I'm not really sure why he left the ranch to me. I just assumed he was going to run the ranch forever."

"Unfortunately," Cash began, "*forever* had a timetable."

He lowered his voice a little as he added, "And we are all very sorry to have lost him."

Right. He had to say that, Ena thought.

"Uh-huh," she finally responded, only because she felt she had to say something.

"As for leaving the ranch to you," Cash continued genially, "you are the only living member of his family."

She wanted to be on her way back to Dallas. "All right, so tell me what I need to sign or do to get this sale moving along," she requested. As far as she was concerned, this was already taking too long.

"What you *need to do*," he informed her, "is to stay here for the next six months."

Ena stared at the man opposite her in disbelief. "You're serious?" she asked, stunned.

Cash nodded. "Absolutely. Those are the terms of your father's will." To prove it, he read the brief section to her.

Ena made an unintelligible noise. "Even from beyond the grave, that man found a way to put the screws to me," she cried.

"In your father's defense, I think that he thought of it as a way to bring you back to your roots," Cash told her.

"My roots," she informed him stubbornly, "are in Dallas."

"That might be," Cash conceded. "But your father saw it differently."

Ena rolled her eyes. "My father saw *everything* differently. He made it his mission in life to contradict every single thing I said or did," she informed him.

Cash did his best to attempt to smooth over this obviously rough patch. "I realize that there was some bad blood between you years ago—"

"There was *always* bad blood between us," she informed the lawyer tersely. "The only reason it wasn't spilled was because my mother—who was a saint, by the way, for putting up with the man—acted as a buffer between us. Once she was gone, there was no one to step in and try to make my father be reasonable—so he wasn't. Everything that ever went wrong was, in his opinion, my fault."

Ena stopped abruptly, catching herself before she could get carried away.

"I'm sorry," she apologized. "My father always had a way of bringing out the worst in me. How long do I have to decide whether or not I'm going to abide by the terms of this will of his?" she asked.

"I'm afraid you have to if you want to keep the ranch," Cash told her.

"So I guess that's the decision before me," she said. "Whether or not I want to keep the ranch. Tough one," she said flippantly. "How long did you say I have before I have to give you my decision?"

Cash stared at her. For the moment, she had managed to stump him.

Chapter Three

Knowing some of the circumstances behind Ena's relationship with her father, Cash cleared his throat and tried to be as diplomatic as possible. "I realize that the situation between you and your father wasn't exactly the best."

Ena suppressed the involuntary harsh laugh that rose to her lips. "I take it that you have a penchant for making understatements, Mr. Taylor."

"Call me Cash." He didn't comment on Ena's observation. "Things aren't always the way that they seem at first glance."

Ena folded her hands before her on the desk. Her knuckles were almost white. "If you're referring to my father," she told the lawyer evenly, "Bruce O'Rourke was *exactly* the way he seemed. Cantankerous, ornery and dead set against everything I ever said or did." She drew back her shoulders, sitting ramrod straight in the chair. "My fate was sealed the day I was born, Mr. Taylor—Cash," she corrected herself before the lawyer could tell her his first name again.

"That's being a little harsh, wouldn't you say?"

"No," she replied stiffly, "I wouldn't. If anything, I'm being sensitive. My father was the harsh one." A dozen memories came at her from all directions, each with its own sharp edges digging into her. Ena winced as she struggled to block them all out. "He never forgave me for being the one who lived," she told Cash quietly.

Cash looked at her, completely in the dark as to her meaning. "I'm sorry?"

She had probably said too much already. But word had a way of getting around in this little town and if he didn't know about her father's tempestuous relationship with her, he would soon. He might as well hear it from her. This way, he'd at least get a semblance of the truth. It was his prerogative to believe her or not.

"I had a twin brother. It turned out that my mother was only strong enough to provide the necessary nourishment and bring one of us to term." She took a deep breath as she regarded her folded hands. "My brother didn't survive the birth process. I did. My father had his heart set on a boy. I was just going to be the consolation prize." She raised her eyes to meet Cash's. "He never got over the fact that I survived while my brother was stillborn. My father spent the rest of his life making me regret that turn of events."

Deeply ingrained diplomacy kept Cash from arguing with Ena's take on the matter. Instead, he said, "Still, he did leave the ranch to you."

"No," she contradicted, "he dangled the ranch in front of me and left me with a condition, which was something he always did." She thought back over the course of her adolescence. "He enjoyed making me jump through hoops—until one day I just stopped jumping."

Over the course of his career, Cash had learned how to read people. Right now, he could anticipate what his late client's daughter was thinking. "I wouldn't advise doing anything hasty, Ms. O'Rourke. Give the terms of your father's will a lot of thought," Cash advised.

"I've already thought it over," Ena informed the lawyer, "and I've decided not to play his game."

Cash's eyes met hers. "Then you're going to let him win?"

Ena looked at the attorney sitting on the other side of the desk. Her brow furrowed. "Excuse me?"

"Well," he began to explain, "from what you've said, your father always made you feel that you were a loser. And if you walk away from the ranch, you'll be forfeiting it, which in effect will be making you a loser. And that, in turn, will be telling your father that he was right about you all along."

Ena scowled at the lawyer. "You're twisting things."

The expression on his smooth face said that he didn't see things that way. "Maybe, in this case," he responded, "I'm able to see things more clearly because I don't have all this past baggage and animosity coloring my perception of things." He slid to the edge of his seat, moving in closer to create an air of confidentiality between them. And then he punctuated his statement with a careless shrug. "I'm just saying…" he told her, his voice trailing off.

He was doing it, Ena thought, irritated. Her father was boxing her into a corner, even though he was no longer walking among the living. Somehow, he was still managing to have the last say.

Ena frowned. As much as she wanted to tell this lawyer what he could do with her father's terms, as well as his will, she knew that Cash was right. If she tore up the will and walked out now, that would be tantamount to giving up—and her father would have managed to ultimately win.

She hated giving him that, even in death.

Blowing out a breath, she faced her father's lawyer with a less-than-happy look.

"I have to stay here for six months?" She asked the question as if each word was excruciatingly painful for her to utter.

"You have to run the ranch for six months," Cash corrected, thinking she might be looking for a loophole. There weren't any.

"Can I delegate the work?" Ena asked, watching the man's face carefully.

"You mean from a distance?" Cash asked. She wanted to oversee the operation from Dallas, he guessed.

"Yes," she said with feeling. "That's exactly what I mean."

"No." The lone word shimmered between them, cloaked in finality. "Your father was very clear about that. He wanted you to be on the ranch while you oversaw the work that needed to be done."

Ena swallowed a guttural sound. It was all she could do to keep from throwing her hands up in frustration. "I don't know anything about running a ranch. My father told me that over and over again," she emphasized. "He deliberately kept me away from the day-to-day process—other than mucking out the stalls. *That* he was more than happy to let me do."

"Obviously he'd had a change of heart about the

matter when he had me write up the will. And anyway," Cash went on, "you have some very capable men working at the Double E. I'm sure that they all would be more than willing to help you."

He was right and that was exactly her point. "So why can't I just tell them to use their judgment and keep the ranch running just the way that they always have?" she asked.

The look on Cash's face was sympathetic. He could see how frustrating all this had to be. "Because your father's will was very specific," he told her.

Ena's laugh was totally without any humor. "Yes, I'll bet. It probably said, 'Keep sticking pins in her side until she bleeds.'"

For the first time since they had sat down together, she saw the lawyer grin. "Not even close," Cash assured her.

She wasn't so sure. The sentiment was there all right, just probably hidden between the lines. "You obviously didn't know my father as well as you thought you did."

"Or maybe you're the one who doesn't know the man, at least not the way he was in his last years. It's been ten years," Cash reminded her. "People change in that amount of time, Ms. O'Rourke."

"Normal people do," Ena agreed. "But not my father. He was as set in his ways as any mountain range. To expect that mountain range to suddenly shift would be incredibly foolish."

"So you're turning your back on the will?" Cash concluded.

"No." She saw that her answer surprised him, so, since he'd been the one who had attempted to talk her out of forfeiting her claim, she explained. "Because you were right about one thing. If I just metaphorically toss this back in my father's very pale face, then he will have won the final battle and I'm not ready to let that happen. So," she continued, taking in a deep breath, "even though it's going to turn my whole life upside down, I'm going to stay on the Double E and work it so that I can meet those terms of his. And when I do, I'm going to sell that burdensome old homestead so fast that it'll make your head spin, Mr. Taylor."

Cash smiled at her. "I believe that at this point I'm beyond the head-spinning stage. Don't forget," he reminded her, "Miss Joan is my step-grandmother. Thanks to her, very little surprises me these days. By the way, she asked me to remind you that if you haven't yet. She's waiting for you to drop by to go see her."

Ena shrugged away the reminder. "I don't want to bother her. She's working."

The expression on the lawyer's face told her that he saw right through her excuse. "You *have* met Miss Joan, right?"

Ena stiffened. She had no idea why he would ask her something like that. He had to know the answer was yes. "Yes, of course I have."

"Then you know that she's *always* working," he reminded her. "I don't think that the woman knows how *not* to work."

If Ena had had any lingering doubts that Cash Taylor was actually related to Miss Joan, that put them all to rest. The man was obviously familiar with the diner owner's stubborn streak, as well as her way of overriding any and all who opposed her no matter what that opposition was rooted in.

Ena inclined her head, conceding the point. "You're right. I guess I'll stop by and see her before I leave town today," she told him, hoping that was enough to table this part of the discussion.

Nodding, Cash smiled and then extended his hand to her. "Well, welcome home, Ms. O'Rourke. I just wish this could be under better circumstances."

"So do I, Counselor. So do I," Ena responded with feeling. "Anything else?"

Cash shook his head. "No, I believe we've covered everything."

Gripping the armrests, Ena pushed herself to her feet, ready to take her leave as quickly as possible. "Then I'll be going now. Thank you for telling me about my father's will—and for your guidance," she added.

Although she silently thought that she could have done *without* his guidance since it made her agree to put up with her father's terms. She was, in essence, playing the game in her father's court. Which would make her victory when it came—and it would—that much sweeter.

She just needed to remember that.

On his feet as well, Cash said with genuine feeling, "My pleasure, Ms. O'Rourke. Here, I'll walk you to the door."

"That's really not necessary," Ena said, attempting to deflect the offer.

"I don't know about that. Miss Joan would give me a tongue-lashing if she found out that I'd forgotten my manners. Besides, one of us needs to stretch their legs," he added with a wink.

The "trip" to the law office's front door was an exceedingly short one. She was standing before it in a matter of seconds. Cash managed to open it one moment earlier, holding it for her.

"And don't forget to swing by Miss Joan's—when

you get the chance," he added politely. "She really would love to see you."

Ena nodded, although she sincerely doubted that Miss Joan would actually *love* to see anyone, especially someone who had walked away from Forever ten years ago. She knew for a fact that Miss Joan had little patience with people who felt that they needed to run away from Forever in order to either make something of themselves or, at the very least, find something more meaningful to do with their lives.

Feeling less than triumphant, Ena got into her sports car and drove the short distance to the diner.

She almost wound up driving *past* the diner. After listening to her father's will being read, she really was *not* in the mood to politely listen to someone tell her what was best for her. Miss Joan was not exactly a shy, retiring flower. But she also knew that offending the woman was not exactly the best course of action. So, at the last minute, Ena backed up her vehicle and pulled into the small parking lot.

Because of the hour, the lot wasn't packed.

Or maybe, Ena mused, business had slacked off. She knew that things like that did happen. She had seen it occur more than a few times during her years living in Dallas. One minute a business seemed to be thriving, even turning people away. The next, that same business was trying to figure out just what had gone wrong and why their patrons had forsaken them and were now frequenting another establishment.

But then those businesses, especially the restaurants, had a great many competitors. It was a toss-up as to which of them could come out on top and lure customers away from the others.

As far back as Ena could remember, Miss Joan had

had no competition. There was only one other establishment in Forever. That was Murphy's, owned and run by three brothers who proudly proclaimed the establishment to be a saloon. The Murphy brothers had a running agreement with Miss Joan. They didn't serve any food—other than pretzels—in their saloon and Miss Joan didn't serve any alcoholic beverages in her diner. That made Miss Joan's diner the only "restaurant" in town.

So if the good citizens of Forever wanted to grab a meal during their workday, they would all need to head out to Miss Joan's. Ena caught herself wishing that the diner were crowded now. That way, she could just pop in, officially tell Miss Joan that she was back in town, then slip quietly out. If there was any extra time, she might possibly tell the woman that she was debating temporarily sticking around in Forever, at least until such time as she met the conditions of her father's will and could sell the ranch.

Although she doubted that was necessary. Miss Joan had a way of knowing things before anyone told her. She just *intuited* them. Some hinted it had something to do with a Cajun ancestor in her family tree, but Ena doubted it. There was just something about the woman that couldn't really be pinpointed. She was just uniquely Miss Joan.

Getting out of her vehicle, Ena slowly approached the diner. She climbed up the three steps leading to the diner's door even more slowly.

Staring at the door, Ena decided that this wasn't one of her better ideas, at least not now. With that, she turned away from the door.

She had made it down all three steps when she heard the diner door behind her opening.

"You waiting for trumpets to herald your entrance

to my diner? Or maybe I should be dropping handfuls of rose petals in your path?"

Ena would have known that voice anywhere. Stiffening her shoulders, she turned around and looked up at the small compact woman with deep hazel eyes and hair the color of not quite muted flame. Miss Joan had caught her in the act of escaping. She should have seen this coming.

"I thought you might be too busy for a visit right now," Ena told her.

Miss Joan continued to stand there, one hand fisted on either side of her small, trim waist as she looked down at the girl she viewed as the newly returned prodigal daughter.

She shook her head. "Ten years and you still haven't learned how to come up with a decent excuse. Not that that's a bad thing," Miss Joan said. "At least they didn't teach you how to lie in Dallas. Well?" she asked expectantly when Ena continued to stand where she was. "Are you posing for a statue? Because if you're not, stop blocking the stairs to my diner. Use them and come in, girl."

Miss Joan didn't raise her voice, but the command was clearly there.

Moving like a queen, Miss Joan turned around and walked back into the diner. Everything about the way she moved clearly said that she expected Ena to follow her inside.

Ena's internal debate was very short-lived. She decided that coming into the diner was far easier than walking away from what was clearly a mandate from Miss Joan.

Ena quickly hurried up the three steps. With each step she took, she told herself that she wasn't going to regret this. After all, she had spoken to Miss Joan hundreds of times before. This would just be another one of those times. Lightning was *not* going to streak across the sky and strike her the moment she entered. She was just paying her respects to an old friend.

A rather scary old friend, she thought as she pushed the diner door open with fingertips that were positively icy.

Chapter Four

"Take a seat at the counter, girl," Miss Joan instructed without sparing Ena so much as a glance over her shoulder.

Miss Joan waved a very thin hand toward an empty stool that just happened to be right in the middle of the counter. It was also directly in front of where the woman usually stood when she was observing the various activities that were going on within her diner.

When Ena complied, Miss Joan got behind the counter and asked, "You still take your coffee black?"

"I do," Ena answered.

Nodding, Miss Joan filled up a cup straight from the urn. The coffee in the cup was hot enough to generate its own cloud directly above the shimmering black liquid. Years of practice had the woman placing the cup and its saucer in front of Ena without spilling so much as a single drop.

"Are you hungry?" Miss Joan asked.

Ena shook her head. "No, ma'am, I'm fine," she answered.

Miss Joan's eyes narrowed as they pinned hers with a penetrating look. "When did you eat last?" she asked.

She should have known that she couldn't get away with such a vague answer. She would have no peace until she gave Miss Joan something a little more specific. "I had something at a drive-through early this morning," she told the woman.

"You're hungry," Miss Joan declared in her no-nonsense voice. "Angel," she called out to the chef she had come to rely on so heavily. "I need an order of two eggs, sunny-side up, two strips of bacon, crisp, and one slice of white toast, buttered." Her eyes met Ena's. "Did I forget anything?"

Ena moved her head from side to side. "No. You never do." It was as much of an observation as it was a compliment.

Other than the fact that Miss Joan's hair looked a little redder than it had when she'd left Forever, the woman hadn't changed a bit, nor had she missed so much as a beat, Ena thought. There was something to be said for that.

Waiting on the order, Miss Joan crossed back to Ena. "You back for good?" the woman asked bluntly, not wasting any time beating around the bush.

She wanted to yell out "No," but instead, she proceeded with caution. "I'm taking it one day at a time."

Miss Joan surprised her by letting the response stand. "That's as good a plan as any," the woman allowed. One of her old-timers seated at the end of the counter called out her name and Miss Joan glared in the man's direction. "Can't you see I'm busy talking to Bruce O'Rourke's prodigal daughter?" Shaking her head, she looked back at Ena. "Some people act as if they were raised by she-wolves and have no idea what it means to have manners."

Just then, Angel placed the order on the counter between the kitchen and the main room. "Your order's ready, Miss Joan," Angel told her.

"I see it, I see it. Keep your shirt on," Miss Joan replied testily. Picking the plate up, she brought it over to Ena and put the meal in front of her beside the half-empty coffee cup. Moving seamlessly, she automatically filled the cup up. "Let me know if there's anything else that you need."

Ena had been debating whether or not to say something from the moment she had finally walked into the diner. She decided that she had nothing to lose. "There is something."

Miss Joan retraced her steps and returned to the center of the counter. She looked at the young woman expectantly. "Okay, go on." But before Ena said a word, Miss Joan held her hand up to temporarily stop her. The man at the end of the counter had apparently leaned in to listen to what was about to be said. "This doesn't concern you, Ed," Miss Joan said sharply. "Drink your coffee." It was an order.

"Yes, ma'am," the old-timer murmured, picking up his cup.

Miss Joan's eyes shifted back to Ena. "All right, go ahead."

Ena pulled her courage to her. "Why didn't you try to find a way to get word to me?" she asked, the question emerging without any preamble.

Miss Joan raised one of her carefully penciled-in eyebrows. "About?"

The woman knew damn well what this was about, Ena thought, exasperated. But because this was Miss Joan, she played along and answered, "My father. And before you say that you didn't know how to reach me, your step-grandson knew where to find me in order to send that letter notifying me about my father's death and the fact that there was a will. We both know that nobody knows *anything* in this town without you knowing it first."

"You're giving me way too much credit, girl," Miss Joan said, deflecting the comment.

"That's not true, Miss Joan, and you and I know it," Ena informed her. Her voice grew even more serious. "Why didn't you let me know my father was dying?"

Miss Joan moved in closer over the counter, lowering her voice. "Because your father didn't want me to let you know."

Anger mingled with frustration flashed through Ena's soul. "The noble warrior, dying alone, was that it?" she asked sarcastically.

Miss Joan didn't react well to sarcasm, but for once, she let it slide. She answered the question honestly. "You left ten years ago and stayed away all that time. Your father didn't want some spark of belated guilt being the reason you came back. Besides," she continued, "your father wanted you to remember him the way he was, not the shell of a man he became just before he died."

Ena stared at Miss Joan. She wasn't sure what to believe. "So it was *vanity* that kept him from getting in touch with me?"

Miss Joan shrugged at Ena's conclusion. "If that's how you want to see it. But I always thought you were smarter than that."

"How else am I supposed to see it?" Ena asked, raising her voice.

Miss Joan looked at her sharply. "Eat your breakfast before it gets cold," she ordered just before finally turning her attention to the man seated at the end of the counter.

Any appetite she might have had was gone now, but Ena knew better than to just walk away without at least eating some of the breakfast in front of her. Miss Joan would take that as an insult, not just to her but also to the woman she had working in her kitchen. Miss Joan had never been big on compliments, but in her own way she was fiercely protective of the people she took under her wing.

So Ena forced herself to eat as much as she could keep safely down, then, when she was certain Miss Joan was otherwise occupied, she quietly slipped away from the counter. Ena left a twenty-dollar bill beside her plate, thinking that would cover breakfast and then some.

She had reached the entrance and had almost made good her getaway when she felt a hand on her arm. Startled, she looked and saw that the hand belonged to a waitress she didn't recognize.

The waitress, a girl who might have barely been out of high school, pressed the twenty she'd left on the counter into her hand. Ena looked at the waitress quizzically.

"Miss Joan told me to tell you that she never said anything about charging for the meal," the waitress told her.

Ena looked down at the twenty. *Damn that woman, always getting in the last word*, she thought. Just like her father.

Out loud, she observed, "I guess she never said a lot of things."

"Do you want me to tell her that?" the waitress asked.

Ena shook her head. "No, never mind. Here," she said, trying to give the money to the waitress. "Consider this a tip."

But the other woman kept her hand tightly closed. "Can't," the waitress protested. "I didn't earn it and Miss Joan wouldn't like me taking money like this for no reason."

With that, the waitress turned on her heel and retreated back into the diner.

Ena sighed. *Looks like we're not in Kansas anymore, Toto*, she thought. Ten years in Dallas had caused her to forget just how frustratingly set in her ways Miss Joan could be.

The next six months were going to be hell.

But that didn't change the fact that Miss Joan's stepgrandson was right. If she walked away from the ranch, her father would have won their final battle. There was no way she was about to allow that to happen. She couldn't bear it.

"Into the valley of death rode the six hundred," Ena murmured under her breath, quoting Tennyson's epic poem "The Charge of the Light Brigade." She felt as if she were going through the motions of reliving the actual events depicted in the poem.

Except that she was determined to come out of this alive and victorious.

"Hey, boss," Roy Bailey, one of the hands working on the Double E, called out into the stable. Mitch was inside working with an orphaned foal that was having a great deal of trouble taking his nourishment from the bottle that was being offered to it. "I think she's back."

"You're going to have to be more specific," Mitch responded, raising his voice while keeping his attention on the foal. "Which *she* are you talking about?"

"He means Mr. Bruce's daughter," Wade answered, speaking up for the other ranch hand. "And from what I can see, she doesn't look all that happy."

"I'm guessing she's had the terms of the will spelled out for her," Mitch said. "Hey, Bailey, take over trying to feed this little guy," he instructed the ranch hand, holding out the bottle to him.

Bailey looked rather reluctant, although the hired hand took the bottle from Mitch. "I'm not good with a bottle," he protested.

"That's not the way I hear it," Mitch said with a laugh. "Just hold the bottle. With any luck, the foal will do the rest," he told Bailey.

Rising to his feet, Mitch dusted off his hands. He stepped out of the stables just as Ena was making her way to the ranch house.

He cut her off before she had a chance to mount the steps leading to the porch. Bailey was right about Ena's appearance, he thought.

Out loud, Mitch observed, "Well, you certainly don't look very happy."

Startled, she looked in his direction. Her expression hardened. "I'm not," she told him.

"I take it that your dad's lawyer told you the terms of the will?"

Mitch put it in the form of a question, but he already knew the answer. She wouldn't have been frowning that way if she had been on the receiving end of news that she welcomed.

"Yes, he did," Ena said grimly.

He looked at her for a long moment. "Is that scowl on your face because you've decided not to stay—or because you have?"

Diplomacy was obviously a lost art out here, Ena thought.

"That's pretty blunt," she observed. "You certainly don't believe in beating around the bush, do you, Mitch?"

"Only when it's fun," he said. Then he sobered and added, "But no, not usually. And not, apparently, in this case." His eyes searched her face, looking for a clue. "So, you haven't told me. Are you staying?" he asked, phrasing his question in another form.

Her eyes narrowed. Was he being cute or was he just toying with her? "Do I have a choice in the matter?"

He spread his arms wide. "You could leave," he reminded her.

"Right," she said sarcastically. "And forfeit my birthright?" she asked, stunned that he would even suggest that.

"Is that important to you?" Mitch asked. He was curious to hear what her response to that would be.

"Honestly?" she asked. When Mitch nodded, she told him, "What's important to me is not letting that old man win."

There was that stubborn spirit of hers again, Mitch thought. "Despite whatever I might have alluded to earlier, I don't really think it matters all that much to him one way or the other," he told her, covertly observing her expression. "The old man is past the point of caring."

"Well, I'm not and it does to me," Ena informed him. "And I'll be damned if he gets to ace me out of something that's been in the family for three generations just because I had the *audacity* to be born a female and not his male heir."

He, for one, thought that her having been born a female was a great boon to the world, and especially to him, but he wasn't about to voice that sentiment to her, at least not right now. It would get him into a lot of hot water for a hell of a whole lot of reasons.

"Just so I'm clear on this, you're going to stay on and run the ranch?" he asked, waiting for a confirmation from her.

Ena closed her eyes. The frustrated sigh came up from the bottom of her very toes. "It certainly looks that way," she replied, opening her eyes again.

If he let himself, he could get lost in those eyes, Mitch thought. He always could.

"You're going to need help," he concluded.

"Ordinarily, I would take that as an insult," she told him. She liked to think of herself as self-sufficient and independent, but she also knew her limitations. "But right now, I have to admit that you're right. I'm going to need help. A *lot* of help. To be perfectly honest, I don't really know the first thing about running a ranch—" She saw him opening his mouth to say something and she got ahead of what she knew he was going to say. "And yes, I know I grew up here, but just because you grow up next to a bakery doesn't mean you have the slightest idea how bread is made. Especially if the baker won't let you into the kitchen."

He looked impressed by the fact that she could admit that. "Best way I know how to get started is to just jump right into the thick of things and start working," he told her. She was looking at him quizzically, so he explained, "There's a foal in the stables whose mama died giving birth to him and he needs to be fed if he has any chance of surviving."

The very abbreviated story unintentionally brought back painful memories for Ena. Her mother hadn't died in childbirth, but her twin had. She could definitely relate to that foal on some level.

"Take me to him," she told Mitch.

Mitch suppressed a smile. He'd been hoping for that sort of reaction from her.

"Right this way, Ms. O'Rourke," he said politely, leading the way into the stable.

The foal was skittish when she came up to him. Ena was slightly uncomfortable as she glanced toward Mitch for guidance.

"Just start talking to him," he told her.

"What am I supposed to say?" Ena asked, at a loss for how to proceed.

Mitch shrugged. He'd never had to think about it before. "Anything that comes to mind. Pretend you're talking to a little kid," he suggested.

But she shook her head. "Still not helping. Not many little kids need an accountant," she pointed out.

He thought for a moment, searching for something she could work with. "Tell him how good-looking he is. Every living creature likes to hear that," he told her.

Ena wasn't sure about that. "Really?" she asked him uncertainly.

"Really." Rather than demonstrate, he thought it best to leave it up to her. "Come on," he coaxed. "You can do it. You know how to talk. I know you do," he insisted. "I've heard you."

Ena looked at him sharply. Was he telling her that he remembered going to school with her? That he'd eavesdropped on her talking to someone? Just how much did he remember? Because she instantly recalled the less-than-flattering memories of all but throwing herself at the mysterious new stud who had walked into her school and her life. She also painfully recollected having him politely ignore each and every one of her passes. If he did remember all those passes that fell by the wayside, then working with him to run the ranch was not an option. She didn't handle humiliation well and she'd worry that he was laughing at her.

"What do you mean by that?" she asked suspiciously, bracing herself.

"Just what I said," he answered innocently. "I've heard you. You talked to me when you came here this morning."

"Oh," she responded, simmering down. "That's what you meant."

"Yes. Why?" Mitch asked. "What did you think I meant?"

"Never mind," Ena told him, waving away the foreman's question.

Taking the bottle from one of the men she gathered was working with Mitch, she turned her attention to the foal. The wobbly colt all but attacked the bottle, sucking on it as if his very life depended on it.

He was probably right, Ena thought. "What a good boy," she murmured to the foal, pleased by the success she was having.

Chapter Five

Mitch stood off to the side of the stall, observing Ena as she fed the foal.

"See, it's coming back to you," Mitch told her. The bottle was empty but the foal was still trying to suck more milk out of it. Drawing closer to Ena and the foal, Mitch took the bottle out of her hand and away from the nursing foal. "You're a natural."

Ena shrugged. "It doesn't take much to hold a bottle. The foal's doing the work. It's not like I'm forcing the liquid down his throat."

Mitch shook his head. He didn't remember her being like this when they were in school together.

"I would have thought that being away from here would have made you less defensive, not more," he said. "There's nothing wrong in accepting a compliment."

"I don't need you to tell me what's right and what's not right," she informed him.

Mitch was not about to get embroiled in an argument, not over something so minor.

"Sorry," he apologized. "I meant no disrespect," he assured her easily. "Nobody is looking to trip you up here."

"I know that," she snapped.

The smile on his face was just this side of tight. She was inches away from an explosion, but for now he kept his peace. "Good. Just so we're clear."

Looking to change the subject, Ena glanced back at the foal. She ran her hand lightly along his back. To her surprise, the foal didn't back away. "What's his name?" she asked Mitch.

The foreman watched her face for a reaction. "I was thinking of calling him Bruce, after your dad," he told her. "Seeing as how he was born seven days after your dad passed on."

Ena's first thought was to say that her father wouldn't have appreciated the sentiment or being linked to the foal. But then she decided that her father *might* have liked that. He had certainly been attuned to anything that had to do with the ranch.

Far more so than anything that ever had to do with her, she thought ruefully.

"Well, maybe he would have liked that after all," she finally told Mitch. "But if this foal grows up to have a stubborn streak a mile wide, you can blame it on his name."

Mitch laughed softly, stroking the foal's back. "Your dad was a very stubborn man," he agreed. "But seeing how hard he had to work to keep this place going, he sort of had to be."

Unlike his laugh, Ena's was depreciating, bordering on almost dismissive.

"You don't have to tell me how hard my father worked. That man made sure he drove his point home about how hard he worked every time he'd lecture me—which was all the time," she underscored.

She was trying to draw him in again, Mitch thought, trying to get him into an argument with her. But he stood firm.

"Everybody's got a different parenting style," Mitch replied.

"That's being rather generous," Ena commented coolly. When he looked at her confused, she elaborated, "To call what he did *style*."

Mitch knew that Bruce O'Rourke could be difficult, but he had also mentored him and in effect became like the father he no longer had. He felt as if he had to speak up in the man's defense.

"Aren't you being just a little hard on him?" Mitch asked her.

Ena's answer was immediate. "Not nearly as hard as he was on me." She said the words almost pugnaciously, as if she were ready to fight Mitch on this.

Mitch debated his next words, then decided that he wasn't speaking out of turn. She needed to know this. If he let it go, he'd be doing both her and Bruce a disservice.

"You know," he told her, stepping away from the foal so that he could have her undivided attention. "Your father was heartbroken when you took off the way you did the day after graduation."

She would have given anything if that were true. But she knew that it wasn't. For some reason that was beyond her comprehension, Mitch was being defensive of her father.

"For him to have been heartbroken," she informed

Mitch stiffly, "he would have had to have a heart. And how do you know what he felt? You weren't even here then."

"Actually, I was," Mitch corrected her. "I came to work for your father the day after we graduated." He remembered seeing her at the ceremony. He doubted that she had taken notice of him. The moment it was all over, he'd rushed off to see her father because he had interviewed for a job with the man a couple of days earlier. "I think we missed each other by a few hours. Your dad seemed pretty distraught when I saw him," he recalled.

Ena frowned. "Now you're just making things up," she accused. "You don't have to speak well of him on my account. As a matter of fact, I'd rather you didn't, because then I'd know you're lying." He was making her father out to be some sensitive, kind man and she knew that the man was far from that. "You forget, I lived with the man for eighteen years and I know *exactly* what he was like."

"Men like your father have a hard time letting their feelings show."

Ena didn't see it that way. "He had no trouble letting his anger show. I never had to guess when he was angry—because he was angry *all* the time."

She couldn't remember *ever* hearing so much as one kind word from her father, or any words of encouragement for that matter. All her father could do was point out her faults—at length.

This was going nowhere, Mitch thought. For now he gave up. Inclining his head, he said, "All right, have it your way."

"It's not *my* way. It was his," she insisted. "Now, if you don't mind, I'd like to table this discussion for the time being. I'm going to go into the house and settle in." Walking out of the stable, she headed back to where she had parked her vehicle.

To her surprise, Mitch walked out of the stable as well and followed her to her car. Turning on her heel, she looked at him, thinking he had some more words of "wisdom" to impart.

"What?" she demanded.

"I thought I'd carry in your suitcases for you," he offered.

His amicable offer caught her off guard and effectively took her edge off. She couldn't very well yell at him after that.

"Suit*case*," she emphasized, opening the trunk. "Not *cases*."

He watched her reach in and take out a compact white carry-on. "I guess you believe in traveling light," he noted.

There was a reason for that. "I only intended to stay a couple of days," she replied. "Apparently that's changed," she added with a sigh of resignation.

Executing a smooth movement, Mitch took the suitcase from her and walked toward the house with it.

"Do you want me to gather all the hands together?" he asked, looking at her over his shoulder.

She didn't understand why he would make that kind of offer. "Why would I want that?"

He thought it was self-explanatory. There were a few new hands here since she'd left, men who had been hired on after he had started working here. "I thought so you could meet them officially."

She supposed that was a good idea, but she wasn't up to that right now. There was one killer of a migraine forming right behind her eyes. Once one of those got going, it didn't stop until it all but consumed her. She had felt it starting in the lawyer's office, right after he had explained the will to her.

The migraine had her father's name on it.

Just like in the old days, Ena thought.

"This is a small town and word spreads fast so I'm guessing that the new *hands* all already know who I am. As for the individual hands, I'll meet them on the job. Best way to get to know someone is by seeing the level of their work." She almost winced when she realized that she had just quoted one of her father's edicts. Damn the man for getting into her head. "But right now, I'm going to go and lie down."

"Not feeling well?" Mitch asked sympathetically.

It almost sounded as if he cared, Ena thought. But why should he? He was probably hoping that she'd take a turn for the worse so that he could get the ranch from her—cheap. She was willing to bet that her father's "foreman" had fancied himself running the place—until he'd heard about the will.

"Sorry to disappoint you, but it's nothing fatal," she told him. She struggled to block the shiver and only partially succeeded. "It just feels that way." Ena saw the tall cowboy looking at her as if he couldn't comprehend what she was saying to him. "I get migraine headaches," she explained. "I realize that a person can't die from that—they just want to. Or at least I do when it goes into high gear like this."

"You take anything for it?" Mitch asked, closing the front door behind them.

"Why? What are you planning on giving me?" She winced again. "Sorry, bad joke. But I can't do any better right now."

Mitch nodded. "I'll bring this into your room," he said, lowering his voice. And then he stopped to consider what he'd just said. "Will you be taking over your father's bedroom?"

She looked at him as if he were crazy. Why would she want to do that? "Oh, lord, no. If I do that, I won't sleep until I get back to Dallas. My father would haunt me if I'm in his room," Ena told the foreman.

Rather than just go along with what she'd just said or gloss over it, Mitch asked, "Then you believe in spirits?"

"Not *spirits*," she corrected. "*Spirit*. Just one. Singular," Ena stressed. "A ghost. If there's a way for my father to come back and haunt me, he'll find it and I'd rather not be camped out in his room when he does. No, I'll just take my old bedroom," she told Mitch. Then she added, "It's the first room on the right at the top of the stairs."

He was already heading up the stairs. "Yes, I know," he told her.

"How?" she asked him, puzzled.

She had never had him over when they were in school together. Because he had in essence rebuffed her advances, there had never been any reason to invite him to her house.

"Your father pointed it out to me," Mitch explained. "Said that way, when he came up at night, you could stand there and look down at him."

Flashes of light were interfering with her ability to see right now, but she tried to stare at Mitch. "He didn't say that," she protested.

"I was there, but have it your way," he told her with a shrug. "I don't intend to mark the first day of our working relationship with an argument."

Our working relationship. That sounded way too structured to her. She didn't want to think of her being here in those terms. As far as she was concerned, this was just a day-to-day thing and if there was any chance she could find a way to change it, sell the ranch and take off, she planned to do it. But only *after* she got rid of this awful brain-numbing migraine.

"We'll talk later," she told him, waving him on his way. "After I get the little drummer boy out of my head," she murmured.

Gripping the wooden handrail, she focused on putting one foot in front of the other until she had finally managed to get herself to her room.

Mitch had reached it before she did and he put her suitcase just inside the door. "Let me know if there's anything that you need."

She waved her hand at him, indicating that he should just go. "What I need," she said with effort, "is not to be here."

The corners of his mouth curved. "Other than that," Mitch qualified.

But she had already closed the door on him, shutting out his words and his presence.

Ena found her way over to the double bed. Gingerly, she lay down on the gray-and-blue comforter. The fact that her room had remained just the way she'd left it registered belatedly somewhere amid the growing throbbing pain.

Shutting her eyes, Ena willed herself to fall asleep.

Unfortunately, her brain wasn't being receptive. She tried pulling the covers over her head, but that didn't help, either.

Neither did the almost imperceptible knock on her door that came almost half an hour later.

Ena stifled a moan. She wanted to pretend she hadn't heard it and not respond, but something told her that the person on the other side of the door would just persist in knocking, so she surrendered.

"Yes?" she asked weakly. Even the sound of her own voice was making the migraine worse.

"Do you mind if I come in?"

It was Mitch, she realized. *Now what?* She sighed, remaining where she was, a prisoner of this throbbing hotbed of pain.

"Might as well," she said in a whisper. "This migraine isn't going anywhere and neither am I."

She heard the door opening. She didn't hear it close. Was that for her protection? Or his?

It wasn't until she finally pried open her eyes that she saw that Mitch was carrying something. Up until this point, she had been doing her best trying to block out everything, including the ranch, all without much success.

He brought the cup over to her bedside, but she wasn't looking at that. She wanted to know why he was here. "What is it?"

Mitch nodded at the mug he was holding. "I thought this might help."

What was he talking about? "*What* might help?" Ena asked. Very slowly, she pulled herself up into a sitting position. The very act threatened to split her head right in half. The pain was also making her nauseous.

"This." He indicated the large mug he was holding. She caught a whiff of something aromatic and warm— tea? She wasn't in the mood for guessing games. Or for tea.

"What is that?" Ena asked, opening her eyes and trying to focus. She thought she saw steam curling from the mug in his hand.

"Something that is going to help make that headache of yours go away," he told her.

She truly doubted that. "Arsenic?"

"Nothing quite that drastic," Mitch assured her with a chuckle.

"Then it won't work," she told him. "Take it away."

Mitch didn't move a muscle. "Give it a try. What do you have to lose?"

"Miss Joan's breakfast."

"I promise this won't make you sick," he coaxed.

"All right, I'll drink it if it'll get rid of you," she muttered, resigned.

Ena took the mug into both her hands. For a moment, she let herself absorb the warmth. It was comforting, but she strongly doubted that whatever was in the mug would do anything to help alleviate the savagery that was going on in her head.

"What is this, really? Chamomile tea?" she asked, looking down at the dark liquid that was shimmering before her.

"No. Just something my mother used to whip up using herbs and a little of this and that for her friends when they had migraines. It's all natural," he assured her.

"So's a coyote, but I wouldn't bring it into my room and pet it," she retorted.

"Just drink it," Mitch urged.

She supposed she had to give it a try since he had gone out of his way to throw this together. But she really had her misgivings that this aromatic brew was going to help. She just hoped that she wasn't going to regret being so trusting.

"This and that?" she echoed.

Sensing that she wasn't going to drink the tea he'd

made without having him elaborate, he gave her the names of the ingredients that his mother had taught him to use.

Ena stared at him. "Are those real names, or are you making things up?" she asked.

"You can look the names up when you feel better. The remedy is something that my mother's mother passed on to her. And, if I'm not mistaken, her mother's mother before that, although I wouldn't swear to that part. All I know is that everyone who ever tried this *tea* had positive results."

"Okay." Ena took a tentative sip and immediately made a face. "Really? Positive results? This tastes awful."

"I didn't say that anyone said it tasted good, only that it worked well." He had a feeling that she needed to think this was her idea, not something he had talked her in to. "Try it or don't try it, it's up to you," Mitch told her. "I'll see you later—or tomorrow."

Ena sat there with the mug in her hand until he had let himself out, closing the door behind him. Then, taking a deep breath, she brought the cup back up to her lips. Still holding her breath, she drank the entire mug in what amounted to one long endless sip.

Finished, she shivered as she struggled to assimilate the bitter brew.

Setting the mug down, she lay back in bed and closed her eyes, sincerely hoping she wasn't going to throw up. Or die.

Chapter Six

It was gone.

Ena was on the verge of drifting off to sleep when she suddenly realized that the killer migraine that had been threatening to take off the top of her head for the last hour had totally disappeared. It was if it had never existed at all.

Ena gingerly raised herself up to a sitting position, afraid that any sudden movement on her part would cause the migraine to return with a vengeance. She held her breath.

But the migraine didn't return at all.

Still worried that this was all just wishful thinking on her part, Ena tested the extent of her "miracle recovery" by slowly moving her head from side to side once, and then again.

Nothing.

She swung her legs off the bed, putting her feet on the floor. Ena slowly stood up. Still nothing.

Although she didn't suffer from migraines frequently, whenever they did come, the migraines hit with the force of a neutron bomb exploding in her head. Every shattered fragment lingered, sometimes for an entire day.

Ena looked at her watch. It had been less than twenty minutes since she'd ingested that mouth-puckering tea concoction that Mitch had brought to her and as odd as it was for her to believe, the tea had eradicated every last bit of her temple-crushing headache.

She felt almost giddy with relief. There was no way, given the short amount of time that had passed, that this was just a coincidence and her migraine hadn't just vanished. Ena had lived through far too many of these episodes to believe that.

Ena went down the stairs, still taking things slowly. Reaching the landing, she looked around for Mitch. She was certain he would be waiting to observe the effects of his mother's magical tea.

A thorough look around the ground floor told her that Mitch wasn't anywhere in the house.

From the house Ena went directly to the stables. Her thinking was that was the last place he had been before bringing her suitcase into the ranch house for her. She wasn't about to say she was looking for him. Ena intended to use the foal as an excuse for her being there, saying that she wanted to see how the colt was doing.

If she wasn't mistaken, the foal needed to be fed every few hours. Mitch had said that it had been born only a few days ago.

Mitch didn't seem to be around. Wade and another ranch hand she didn't recognize were the only ones in the stables.

Disappointed, Ena asked Wade, "Have you seen Mitch around anywhere?"

Rather than give her a verbal answer, Wade pointed directly behind her. Startled, Ena spun around on her heel and found herself looking up into Mitch's face.

His gleaming white teeth almost blinded her. He looked extremely satisfied to find her there. "I see that my mother's remedy worked."

Ordinarily, she would have made some sort of an attempt to deny the assumption or even say something disparaging about the bitter drink. But truthfully, she felt far too good about recovering from what she had been sure was going to be an utterly disabling headache. When they hit, her migraines usually laid her low for at least half a day, if not longer.

Her enthusiasm bubbled over, causing her to declare, "It's fantastic." And then she had a question for him, just to make sure that this wasn't some sort of fluke occurrence.

"Does that *remedy* work like this every time?" she asked. There was still a little skepticism in her voice.

"That's what I hear from everyone who's ever tried it," he told her.

She wanted to explore this further. "And you just used herbs and roots and—whatever those other ingredients you said were?" she asked, unable to remember the exact names he had used.

"I did," Mitch confirmed. Then, keeping a straight face, he added, "Plus a little bit of fairy dust mixed in for good measure just at the end."

Ena stopped short, staring at him. Was there another additive in that mixture he hadn't mentioned before? One that wasn't legal? Her concern spiked.

"You're kidding," she cried, her eyes trained on his face.

He let her go on believing the scenario she had conjured up for half a second before saying, "Yes, I'm kidding. My mother used things that she grew in her garden. Herbs that, for the most part, are plentiful and can be easily found around here." Mitch took out a packet from his hip pocket and handed it to her. "The next migraine you get, you'll be ready for it," he promised. "Just dissolve it in hot water."

Ena studied the packet he'd handed her. It looked rather harmless, but who knew? Still, she wanted to believe that he wouldn't put her on.

"And what's in here can be readily found in the area?" she asked.

"Absolutely. All the ingredients grow like weeds around here. Trust me." Mitch saw the momentary doubt that came into her eyes. "And not the kind of weed that's illegal. Nobody would arrest you for *holding* if they found this on you. It just looks like you're about to brew some tea—which you would be if you find yourself having another one of those crippling headaches."

Ena held the packet up, examining it carefully. Another thought hit her. "Did your mother ever try to sell this?"

"You mean to her friends?" Mitch questioned. When Ena nodded, he answered, "No, why would she do that? She would have gladly shared her knowledge. Anyone could have gathered the ingredients, ground them up and made their own serviceable tea."

He was giving people too much credit, she thought. "These might grow everywhere, but not everyone can figure out how much to use and which specimens to pick to make that tea."

Ena no longer seemed leery. Mitch saw the thoughtful look crossing her face. She was going somewhere with this.

"What are you getting at?" he asked her.

She held up the packet. "Have you ever thought of marketing this?"

Mitch laughed, amused. Maybe she *didn't* know what went into running a ranch like this one. "When?" he asked. "In my spare time?"

To his surprise, Ena nodded. "It might be something to think about."

"I'm a cowboy. This is what I know," Mitch told her, gesturing around the stable. "Thanks to your dad," he added. It was only right to give credit where it was due. If Bruce O'Rourke hadn't taken him under his wing when he had, who knew where he would be now?

Mitch saw the frown on Ena's face. "That might not be what you want to hear, but it's true. Just like it's true that I wouldn't have the first *idea* how to begin mass producing what's in that packet—or how to let people know about it."

Those were all things that she knew about. "That could all be worked out," Ena told him, not willing to give the idea up just yet.

Although he liked hearing her be optimistic, this wasn't something he had time for.

"Right now I—*we*," he corrected, ever mindful of the part she played in all this, "have a ranch to run. A lot of people depend on this place to earn a living. Your dad knew that and I'm not about to let him down."

Ena nodded grimly. She could respect that. She just wished that it didn't involve her father, even in spirit. But right now, she wasn't about to ruin the fact that she felt like a woman who had been reborn, thanks to his mother's miracle remedy, so she let his comment go.

"All right," Ena said gamely, "what do you want me to do?"

The question surprised him. He would have expected her to start issuing orders, even if she didn't have the slightest clue what needed to be done. She had been away from this for ten years, and according to what she'd said, her father had never allowed her to be involved in running the ranch to begin with. That she seemed apparently willing to take a back seat—at least for now—gave him hope that they would be able to work well together.

It was a far cry from the woman who had burst onto the scene this morning.

He didn't have to think to answer her question. "Off the top of my head, the stalls need cleaning, the feed needs to be distributed and that foal you were feeding earlier is hungry again."

"You mean Bruce?" she asked, knowing full well that he did.

"Yes," Mitch answered, obliging her, "I'm talking about Bruce."

She smiled slowly, thinking of the foal she had made a connection with. "I guess I can manage that." She looked around. "Where's his bottle?"

Mitch sent one of the hands, Billy, to fill and retrieve the bottle for her. That done, he began to leave the foal's stall.

Ena had thought he was going to stay here with her. "Where are you going?"

"Remember those other chores I just mentioned that needed doing? They're not going to do themselves, plus there's other things to see to. And you've got this," he said with just the right touch of confidence. He didn't want to oversell it in case it blew up on him.

"Yes, I've got this," she echoed just as Billy returned with a full bottle for the foal.

Mitch flashed a smile at her a second before he walked out.

She took the bottle Billy held out to her, nodding her thanks.

"Okay, Bruce," Ena said, still feeling rather strange to be using her father's name in reference to the foal. "Let's get to it. I've always wanted to know what it felt like to have you eating out of my hand, Bruce."

"Ma'am?" the cowboy asked just as he was about to leave the stall and join Mitch.

Ena waved away his puzzled look. "Just a private joke. It's Billy, right?" she asked, looking at the cowboy she judged to be a few years younger than she was.

"Yes, ma'am." As an afterthought, the cowboy removed his hat and held it in his hand. "Billy Pierce."

"Nice to meet you, Billy Pierce," she said warmly. "Have you been working here long?"

"Just a little over two years, ma'am." He looked at her with genuine sympathy. "I am sorry about your dad passing."

He had to say that, Ena thought. But she wasn't about to pull the young cowboy into the resentment she was experiencing, so she merely acknowledged his comment by saying "Thanks." When the hired hand continued to stand there, she felt compelled to ask, "Is there something else, Billy?"

Billy nodded his shaggy blond head. "Your dad was a good boss to work for."

That she hadn't been expecting. She had never thought of her father as being either good or fair. She truthfully had never thought of her father interacting with anyone else outside of her, and her mother while Edith O'Rourke had been alive. She had just assumed that he had been hard as nails with everyone.

"So I'm told," Ena replied quietly. "You'd better get going and do whatever Mitch has you doing," she gently prodded the young man.

The startled look on Billy's face told her that he had momentarily forgotten about that. "Oh, right," Billy responded. With that, he quickly left the stall.

"Looks like it's just you and me, Bruce," she said to the foal. The colt was busy going at the bottle she held in her hand, madly sucking at its contents. "I really wish that Mitch had given you a different name. You're way too cute to be called *Bruce*."

The foal made a noise, as if he agreed with her assessment.

The timing was so perfect that she had to laugh despite herself. Ena ran her hand along the foal's neck, petting the animal.

"Don't worry about the name, it doesn't matter. I have a feeling that we're going to be fast friends after the dust settles," she told the foal. "So, what do you think?"

It was probably her imagination, but she could have sworn that the foal made eye contact with her for a moment, then whinnied as if he were in agreement with her judgment.

Ena nodded. "We'll see, boy. We'll see," she promised.

"So, how's it going?" Mitch asked, popping in for a moment just in time to see that the foal had finished feeding.

"He ate everything," she announced, then held up the empty bottle to prove her point to him. "Okay, what's next on the agenda?"

He smiled at the foal. He knew he shouldn't but he thought of the foal as more of a pet than just another horse. "Now I take the foal with me and see if I can get Paulina to adopt him."

"Paulina?" she echoed, confused. What was he talking about?

The stable door was open. He stepped over to the side so that she had a better view of the mare he was talking about.

"That dapple-gray mare over there." Mitch pointed to the horse on the far side of the corral. "She lost her foal in the spring. Breech birth, almost lost them both," he told her. "The vet had to make a quick choice."

"Bet my father didn't like losing a foal," Ena commented. It wasn't actually a guess. She knew how her father thought.

"He didn't," Mitch replied, "but he told the doc that he understood about her making a choice and he appreciated her saving Paulina."

She stared at him, amazed. "My father said that?" she asked incredulously. That didn't sound a thing like the man she'd known. "You sure it was him? You don't have him confused with someone else?"

"I'm sure," Mitch told her. "I told you, your father changed. Maybe having you take off that way when you did made him reevaluate the way he'd been doing things up to that point."

Ena snorted. "Now I know you have him confused with someone else. My father *never* thought he was in the wrong. Besides, if my father had this big epiphany the way you claim he did, why didn't he try to find me? I didn't disappear off the face of the earth," she stated. "I even sent him a couple of Christmas cards those first two years so he wouldn't think that I was dead."

Mitch bit the inside of his lip. He really wanted to say something, but he knew that it was too soon for that. Saying it might make her turn on her heel and retreat. And right now, he needed her to stay, as per the will, because that was the only way she would be able to eventually sell the ranch—or hold on to it if she changed her mind about its disposal. He was hoping for the latter.

Either way, she was the one who needed to do this.

"You want to come with me while I make the introductions between Paulina and Bruce?" he asked. "I might need a little help in keeping Bruce calm and he really seems to have taken to you."

Ena nodded. She liked being part of the process, she thought. "Sure. What do you want me to do?"

"Just keep the colt steady while I get this rope on him," he requested. Making a loop to slip over the foal's head, Mitch talked to the animal in a calm, gentle voice the entire time. "This isn't going to hurt a bit, Bruce. We just want to make sure you don't run off before you get to meet your new mama. That all right with you, boy?"

Ena listened to Mitch talking to the foal as if Bruce were capable of taking in each word. "You think he understands you?" she asked the foreman skeptically.

"Maybe not the words," Mitch allowed. "But definitely the tone. And by and by, he'll pick up on the words, as well," he told her confidently. "You just have to remember to keep talking to him as if he understands every word—and eventually, he will," he concluded. Mitch glanced at her, making a decision. He'd been vacillating about this over the course of the day, ever since she'd shown up. But she needed to hear this. She needed to appreciate the man that her father was. "Your dad taught me that," he told Ena.

"Uh-huh," she murmured, humoring Mitch.

She was making agreeable noises, but he wasn't fooled. Still, if he said it often enough, Mitch thought, he'd get her to believe it eventually, just like with the foal.

Chapter Seven

The mare, Paulina, seemed to have her doubts about nursing the foal that had been presented to her. At first, she wouldn't have anything to do with Bruce, but the foal was nothing if not persistent. Each time the mare nudged him aside, the foal just kept coming at her.

For her part, Ena did her best to bring the two animals together, coaxing the mare into accepting the barely two-week-old colt.

Eventually, just before she was about to throw up her hands and give up, Ena's persistence paid off. Expecting another repeat performance by the mare in which Paulina pushed the foal away, she was extremely pleased when Paulina *didn't* kick the foal aside the way she had done several other times.

"I *knew* you'd come around eventually," Ena told the mare. "Couldn't resist that sad little face forever, could you?" she asked. The mare seemed to look at her, then looked away, giving her attention to Bruce. "That's okay, you don't have to say anything. I understand where you're coming from." Ena laughed softly. "The little guy got to me, too."

"Is she answering you?" Mitch asked, grinning as he walked up behind her.

It took everything Ena had not to jump when she heard the sound of his voice. She had been totally sure that she was alone with the mare and the foal.

"Have you ever thought of investing in a pair of spurs?" she asked.

She actually sounded serious when she asked the question, which in turn confused him. "Why?" he asked.

"Because that way you couldn't sneak up on a person," she told him.

Now it made sense. "I wasn't aware that I was doing that," Mitch told her.

"You were," she assured him. Looking at the mare and foal, she noted that neither had reacted to Mitch's presence. They obviously had stronger nerves than she did. Either that or they were just comfortable around him. "I never hear you coming," she accused.

"Sorry. I'll try to walk louder," Mitch promised, amused.

She didn't appreciate Mitch's comment, or his amusement. "Just clear your throat or make some kind of other noise when you're coming up behind me. That's all I ask."

Mitch winked at her, instantly causing a knot to form in her stomach.

"I'll cough," he told her. Then he turned his attention to the real reason he had swung by her. "So, how's the bonding session going? Any luck?"

Ena nodded. "I think that Bruce may have had a little breakthrough with his new mother. The last time he came up to nurse, Paulina didn't kick him away," she told Mitch proudly.

"Hey, that *is* progress. Great work," he declared, congratulating her. "I didn't think we'd get anywhere with Paulina for at least a couple of days." Mitch grinned. "Good thing for Bruce that you came home when you did." When he saw the look on Ena's face when he said that, Mitch had a feeling he knew where he had gone wrong. "You don't think of this as being your home, do you?"

Rather than saying yes or no, she raised her chin defensively. "Home is my apartment in Dallas," she told him. "This, the ranch, is just my birthplace."

"Well, whatever you choose to call it, you coming back here at this time saved me a lot of work," he told her. "Paulina tends not to be all that pliable," Mitch confided. Then he said warmly, "Thanks."

Granted she was secretly proud of herself, but admitting that made her seem somehow vulnerable in her own eyes. So she dismissed his compliment. "I didn't really do anything. It's just nature's way of filling a vacuum."

Mitch could only shake his head. "You are a really hard woman to give a compliment to, you know that?"

Ena handed over the rope that he had put around the foal's neck. "Watching this little guy eat made me realize how hungry I was. I'm going in to see if I can scour up something to eat," she told Mitch, walking away from the mare and what appeared to be the mare's newly adopted foal.

Mitch watched her go. He was about to tell her that

she didn't need to *scour* anything, because when he had gone in to check, The housekeeper, Felicity, was preparing a fried-chicken dinner. She'd probably finished by now and most likely was waiting on "the new boss lady" to come in.

But that was an experience she needed to have firsthand, he thought. So he let Ena go to the ranch house while he got the new "mother" and her foster colt bedded down for the night.

The second Ena walked in through the door, she could smell it. Someone had cooked something.

Chicken?

Had Mitch prepared dinner for them while she'd been busy with the foal and his new "mother"? If that were the case, why hadn't he said anything to her?

She was on her way to the kitchen by way of the dining room when she stopped in her tracks.

The table was formally set.

Had Mitch done that, too? He didn't strike her as someone who would do something like that, not formally at least. He struck her more of the anything-goes type, which meant that she'd have to get her own silverware and dinner plate.

By now she caught another scent. Flowers? No, she detected lilacs, which had to be a cologne. Not the kind that doubled as an aftershave lotion.

Had he brought in a woman to do the cooking?

Ena wasn't sure what to expect as she walked toward the kitchen. While her mother had been alive, all the meals had always been prepared by her. After her mother had passed away, her father had a series of housekeepers who did the cooking and cleaning.

None of them lasted longer than three months. Most

handed in their notices sooner, unable to put up with the demands that her father always issued. When she'd walked in the front door, Ena had been ready to take over the kitchen despite the long day she had put in.

But it didn't look as if she had to.

Just as she was about to troop into the kitchen to find exactly who was behind this scent that had come wafting in to greet her, Ena all but collided with a small compact-looking woman, standing no taller than five foot one.

The woman wore her salt-and-pepper hair up in some sort of hairstyle she'd fashioned that looked like it was half a twist, half a bun. Judging from the dusting of flour that was on the top of her blouse and apron, the woman Ena had narrowly avoided tripping over was the source of not just the cologne but the delicious aroma tempting her, as well.

The woman was carrying out a platter filled with fried chicken pieces.

"Ah, you are here at last," the woman declared with latent satisfaction. "The food was not going to remain warm much longer. Sit," she ordered, gesturing at the place setting at the head of the table.

Ena didn't recognize this miniature tyrant of a woman at all. If she was one of the housekeepers her father had gone through, she had no recollection of her.

Looking at her, Ena said, "And you are…?"

"Busy," the woman responded crisply. "And you will be underfoot if you come into my kitchen." She nodded toward the front door. "Mr. Mitch should be here any minute. With the others," the housekeeper added.

"The others?" Ena repeated, confused. "What others?" she asked.

"The men who work on the ranch, of course," the woman told her.

Of course? There was no *of course* about it. The scenario the woman was describing was a far cry from the almost solitary meals that she had taken in this room with her father the last two years before she'd left.

"Don't they eat in the bunkhouse?" Ena asked, still confused.

"Mr. Bruce said it would be easier for me if everyone ate in here. That was why he had this big table made."

Now that the woman mentioned it, Ena noted that the dining room table was close to one and a half times larger than the one that had been there the last time she had eaten in this room.

"I see you've met Felicity," Mitch said, walking in. "Dinner smells great, Felicity," he told the housekeeper.

Felicity looked unfazed by the compliment. "It tastes even better if you eat it warm."

Ena stared as Mitch took his seat to the right of her chair. She wasn't accustomed to having a foreman eat with her, much less having all the hired hands piling in, as well. "When did all this happen?" she asked, trying to wrap her head around the fact that, according to the housekeeper, this had been her father's idea.

"A few years back." He saw the skeptical expression on Ena's face. He had a feeling he knew what she was thinking. That her father hadn't been behind the suggestion. "I told you your father had changed," Mitch reminded her.

"Was this your idea?" Ena asked, watching as the ranch hands filed in and took their seats around the table.

He wasn't going to tell her that he'd had nothing to do with it, Mitch thought. "Let's just say it was a joint idea, one that your dad agreed only made sense." He could see that she had more questions for him. He second-guessed her. "Your dad saw the advantages of a good meal being the easiest way to keep his men working like well-oiled machines. And Felicity's meals were fantastic," he added. "So if Felicity had to cook for everyone, everyone might as well be in the same room to eat those meals. That made it easier on Felicity." Mitch looked around the table. "Dig in, men. We've got a big day ahead of us tomorrow," he told them.

"Every day's a big day," Wade said as Mitch's lead ranch hand helped himself to several big pieces of Felicity's fried chicken.

Ena's brow furrowed. "What's tomorrow?" she asked, looking from Wade to Mitch.

"Wednesday," Mitch answered simply.

"What he means to say is that every day really *is* a big day." Billy spoke up, trying to make the foreman's comment less mysterious.

"That's just his way of keeping the rest of us from slacking off," Wade told her in between sinking his teeth into the chicken thigh he had speared.

"Why don't you try the mashed potatoes?" Mitch urged, holding out a big serving bowl toward Ena. "In case you didn't know, Felicity makes the best mashed potatoes around," he told her.

How could she know? Ena wanted to ask. She hadn't even known about Felicity until just now.

"It's true," Billy confirmed eagerly, jumping into what he thought was a conversation. "Even better than my mama's."

"You didn't have a mama," one of the other ranch hands teased. "Everyone knows you were hatched out of an egg."

"That's enough," Mitch announced forcefully. "I'm sure that Miss O'Rourke doesn't want to hear you all behaving like a bunch of schoolboys. Do you?" he asked, looking toward Ena for backup.

If she were being honest with herself, Ena wasn't sure if she felt the hired hands' behavior was irritating or entertaining. It was certainly a far cry from what she remembered meals being like when it was just her father and her.

Back then, the air was either filled with recriminations all surrounding her behavior or it was filled with silence because she couldn't find a topic that was safe to broach to her father without hearing any criticism. Ena liked neither, especially not the criticism.

Deciding it was safer to be easygoing, Ena said, "I don't mind."

Her answer immediately won over every man at the table. They all grinned at her almost in unison—and then they all started talking at once, asking her questions, offering comments and information.

Some also told her which of the horses might be ready to be auctioned off and which of the stallions should be kept as breeding stock.

Ena did her best to try to keep everything that was being said at the table straight, but it was all too easy to just lose the thread of what someone was saying, or who was saying it.

By the time dinner was over and the hired hands finally all took their leave, going to the bunkhouse, Ena felt as if her brain were exploding. Not the way it had when she was having a migraine, but it was still being overtaxed.

The expression on Mitch's face when he looked at

her was nothing if not sympathetic. And then he smiled at her. "Worn-out yet?"

"Oh, I'm way past worn-out," Ena told him. She really hated admitting a weakness, or appearing vulnerable. But she felt that on some level, she and Mitch had a bond. So she asked, "Is it like this all the time?"

"This was a slow day," he replied.

Her eyes widened like cornflowers searching for sunlight. "You're kidding."

"Maybe just a little," he admitted, trying to put her at ease, at least to some degree. "But not nearly as much as you'd like me to be. Ranching isn't for sissies," he told her. Then he waited a beat before adding, "That's something else your dad liked to say."

"Yes, I'm familiar with that saying of his," she replied, her face clouding over. "Do you make a habit of quoting my father?"

Maybe he'd overstepped here, but since he had taken that step, he couldn't retreat. That would be counterproductive.

"Only if the occasion calls for it," he told her. "I guess I just wanted you to appreciate the man your father was. He changed from the image you've been carrying around in your head," he explained. "He was a man who decided to take a chance on an eighteen-year-old orphan when he didn't have to—and all common sense told him not to."

He saw her mouth harden just a bit around her jawline and her eyes flash.

"Too bad he didn't want to do that with the daughter he *did* have," Ena murmured.

Abruptly, she pushed her chair back from the table and stood up. Instead of heading for the stairs, the way he thought she would, Mitch saw her heading toward the kitchen. Thinking he might have to avert a situation in the making, he quickly hurried after her.

"That was a very good meal, Felicity," he heard her say to the housekeeper. "I enjoyed it a lot."

The woman turned her head in Ena's direction, her expression ambiguous. And then she smiled at her. "It was my pleasure, Miss Ena," she told the young woman with feeling.

"How long did you work for my father?" Ena asked.

Felicity didn't have to pause to answer. "Eight years."

"You stayed with him for eight whole years?" Ena asked, stunned.

"Yes, I did," the housekeeper replied without any hesitation.

"That's amazing," Ena marveled.

Felicity didn't see what the big mystery was. "Mr. Bruce paid well and he was a good man to work for. He was hard, but he was also fair."

Ena had to admit that she was nothing short of amazed.

The housekeeper wasn't the first one to call her father a good man or say that he was a fair man to work for. Had her father actually undergone some sort of earthshaking rebirth in his later years? Because no one would have ever referred to Bruce O'Rourke as being *good* back when she had lived with him.

She felt almost angry that he had changed this much in his later years—because her mother hadn't been the beneficiary of this miraculous personality change. He had been this really difficult man to deal with back in those days. While Ena was happy that other people found him a good, decent man to work for, she was highly resentful that her father hadn't come around this way while her mother was still alive.

Ena felt tears forming.

Bruce O'Rourke had cheated her mother, Ena thought bitterly. This was just one more thing that she couldn't forgive her father for.

Chapter Eight

Ena hated having to be in a position where she was forced to make excuses. Doing so brought back painfully uncomfortable memories. Suddenly, she was an adolescent, standing before her father and explaining why she had done, or had not done, something. Which was why she avoided the entire scenario if she possibly could.

But she couldn't this time. Couldn't avoid the call she was going to have to make to Jay Whittaker at her firm in Dallas.

Whittaker wasn't exactly her boss so much as he was the senior partner in the accounting firm where she had worked ever since she had graduated from college. But even though he wasn't her boss, she always had the feeling that the vastly competitive man was persistently watching her, waiting for her to slip up and make some sort of mistake. It wasn't anything he

had ever actually said to her as much as it was the attitude he seemed to exude. He enjoyed bullying people.
It made him feel important.

But Ena knew that the longer she put off calling
Whittaker, the longer the call and its outcome loomed
over her.

So the following morning, right after spending a
restless night followed by breakfast she couldn't really
get down, she put in a call to the Dallas office. It was
8:20 a.m., the time when Whittaker always showed up
in the morning. She knew it was because he liked getting the jump on the people he worked with.

Sitting in the small crowded room her father used to
call his den, Ena listened to the phone she'd dialed on
her father's landline ring.

The phone on the other end was picked up after two
rings. Ena willed the knot in her stomach to go away.

"Mr. Whittaker, it's Ena—" she began, only to have
the scratchy-sounding voice belonging to Jay Whittaker cut her off.

"When can I expect you back?" Whittaker asked
bluntly without any polite exchange between them.
"Friday?"

Typical, she thought before trying again. "No, I'm
afraid not—"

"What do you mean *afraid*?" Whittaker asked, in-
terrupting her again.

Whittaker was accustomed to firing out questions
rapidly and getting back answers the same way. Ena
was certain that the man had never had a leisurely conversation in his life.

Putting the call on speakerphone, she wearily attempted to explain, "My father had an unexpected
clause in his will—"

"What kind of clause?" Whittaker asked her impatiently.

"The kind that is going to wind up making me stay here for the next six months," she answered through clenched teeth.

As much as she didn't like being controlled by her father or being forced to stay here in order to comply with the will, Ena liked having to explain herself to Whittaker even less.

"Six months?" The base of the landline all but vibrated from the impact of his high-pitched voice. Ena was just grateful she wasn't holding the receiver against her ear.

Ignoring the man's very obvious display of anger, Ena plowed straight to her point. "I'm going to have to request a leave of absence."

"Well, I'm sorry," Whittaker said in a tone that told her that he was anything *but* sorry, "but you can't ask for one out of the blue. The firm can't—"

She didn't wait for him to finish. "You can call it a family emergency," she informed him. "I have enough vacation time accrued over the last six years to actually cover the time I'm going to need," she pointed out, her voice growing in strength.

The one thing she hated more than having to explain herself was having to ask for a favor. But strictly speaking, this couldn't be called that.

Only Whittaker would think of it in those terms.

"And you expect your job to just be here *waiting* for you once this so-called *emergency* of yours is over with, is that it?" Whittaker asked, a nasty edge to his voice.

Ena tried another approach. She really didn't want to make waves. In general, the firm had been good to her. Whittaker was the only one who had ever been difficult to deal with.

"I can go over some of the work that needs to be done from here. I can work on it in the evening and email it to the office. My assistant at the firm can handle the rest," she assured Whittaker. "Don't worry, the work will be covered."

Whittaker sounded far from placated. Or maybe he just wanted to use this as an excuse to get her out of the way, Ena thought as she heard him say, "I'll have to bring this to Mr. Blackwell's attention."

"I realize that. But you don't have to." Before he could say anything to contradict her, Ena told him, "I'm going to be making a formal request for this leave and sending it to Mr. Blackwell as soon as I get off this phone."

That temporarily took the wind out of the other man's sails. Whittaker made a disgruntled noise. "You realize that the reason you were hired ahead of the other applicants was because you didn't have any baggage. We thought that would prevent this sort of thing from happening and hampering the company."

"The firm isn't being hampered. It's just being mildly inconvenienced," she told him firmly. "Believe me, I'm not happy about this."

"That makes two of us," Whittaker bit off. He made another aggravated sound, then told her, "I want regular updates from you. I'll have one of the assistants send out one of your accounts to you the second I clear this with Mr. Blackwell."

With that, Ena heard the connection terminate. Swallowing a few choice words, she leaned back in her chair.

"Nice guy," Mitch said, coming into the den. "He your boss?"

Startled, she turned her chair in Mitch's direction. She hadn't realized anyone was there. She still wasn't getting used to him materializing out of nowhere.

"He thinks he is," she said, frowning. "Whittaker's in charge of one group. I have another. Nobody's really the *boss* except for Aaron Blackwell, the man who started the firm," she told Mitch. She pushed her chair back and rose to her feet. "I didn't realize that you were eavesdropping."

"I wasn't. You had that guy on speakerphone and I think the horses in the stable heard him," Mitch quipped. "Sounds like a charmer," he commented. "He always that pleasant?"

"Even before his wife left him," Ena replied.

"Well, I can definitely see why his wife left him," Mitch commented. "Listen, I know your dad's will said you had to work on the ranch for six months, but it didn't specifically say *constantly*."

She looked at him as they walked out of the house. "What are you getting at?"

"Maybe you could go to Dallas a couple of days a week, hold that guy's hand, so to speak, if you need to. I wouldn't want to see you get fired," he told her.

What he meant was that he didn't want to see her self-esteem take a beating, even though the whole idea behind Bruce O'Rourke's will was to get his daughter to change her mind about running the ranch rather than selling it.

"Whittaker can't fire me," she told Mitch.

He wondered if she was just saying that because the truth embarrassed her.

"He certainly sounded as if he thought he could," Mitch said.

"Well, he can't. Especially since I do have all that

vacation time accrued." She slanted a glance toward Mitch. He meant well and she appreciated that. "But thanks for the thought," she murmured.

"Don't mention it," he told her. "Why don't you come to the stable and see how Bruce and his new *mother* are doing?" he urged.

Because of the way her mind had been trained to work, anticipating the worst, Ena immediately thought something had gone wrong. "Is there a problem?"

The smile on his face alleviated her initial anxiety. "On the contrary, I think you helped fill a need in both their lives."

"You were the one who suggested it," she reminded him. She didn't want him to think she could be manipulated with empty flattery.

"I did," he agreed, "but you were the one who kept encouraging the little guy to keep trying even after he'd been rejected over and over again."

She looked at him in surprise. "How would you know that?"

"I have my spies," he teased. And then he said, "Billy told me."

She jumped to what was, to her, the natural conclusion. "You had him watching me?"

"No," Mitch replied patiently, "*he* made that choice on his own. If you ask me, I think that Billy has a crush on you."

She thought Mitch was kidding, then realized he wasn't. Ena sighed. That was all she needed: to have a wet-behind-the-ears cowboy following her around like a puppy dog.

"Well, I didn't ask," she informed Mitch, dismissing the entire incident.

"Point taken," the foreman replied with a good-natured grin.

Ena picked up her pace as she walked toward the stables. Despite everything, she was eager to see for herself how well the foal was getting along with his newfound "mother." She silently admitted that she needed that sort of boost to her frame of mind, which was at the moment, despite what she had said, at a low point thanks to Whittaker. Not to mention the feeling that she was in over her head when it came to the ranch.

The second she walked into the stall, she was saw that the mare was indeed allowing the foal to nurse. And when Paulina decided that her new foal had had enough, she made her wishes known by forcefully nudging the colt aside.

Mitch watched in silence right beside Ena.

"No matter what you say, that's all thanks to you," he finally told her. He could tell that compliments made her uncomfortable, so he dropped it at that. "Seen enough?"

Obviously, that was her cue to leave, Ena thought, so she began to walk out again. "Yes. What do you have in mind now?"

For the briefest of seconds, her question gave birth to an entirely different response than he was free to make. Because what he had in mind was nothing he was able to actually say.

So instead, he said, "Nothing out of the ordinary. Just the same old routine as yesterday." And then he thought of an alternative. "Unless you feel like helping fix a part of the fence that's just about ready to fall apart."

"Sure," she told him almost eagerly. "Where is this fence that's on the verge of crumbling?"

His suggestion had been an offhanded comment,

thrown in on a whim, nothing more. He hadn't expected her to respond in such a positive way.

"It's just at the end of the northern pasture." Mitch looked at her somewhat uncertainly. "You sure you want to do this?"

"I wouldn't have asked if I didn't. I like working with my hands," she told him.

Mitch picked up one of her hands and carefully examined it. It was just as he'd thought.

"Your skin's smooth and your nails aren't broken. You'll forgive me if I have my doubts about your claim about working with your hands."

She tossed her head, sending her blond hair flying over her shoulders. "Just take me to what you need fixed and prepare to eat your words, Parnell."

For her to be that confident in her abilities could only mean one thing. "So your dad did have you working on the ranch," Mitch concluded.

"No," she contradicted. "I took a woodworking class after hours at the high school. My father made it clear that he didn't think I could do anything. I took that class just to show my father that I actually *could* be handy."

"And did you show him?" he asked as they headed toward his pickup truck. The back was loaded with posts, planks of wood and the tools that were necessary to do the required work.

Ena shrugged in response to his question. "I never got the chance. I figured I'd do it the day after graduation. But then there was this one last knock-down, drag-out argument between us just before the graduation ceremony." Her face clouded over as she relived every single detail in her head. "I took off the next day."

"Maybe you should have waited," Mitch said.

"Things might have turned out differently between the two of you if you had."

"I really doubt it," she said, climbing into the passenger side of the cab. She knew he was thinking about the way her father had supposedly changed over these last ten years. "I think he changed because you came into his life."

Mitch started up the truck, then looked at her, stunned. "Me? No, I think you got that wrong." As a matter of fact, he was quite certain of it.

But Ena shook her head. "I don't think so. You turned out to be the son he had always wanted. Once you came into his life, from what you've said, it looks to me that he started to be less angry at the world and started turning into a human being."

But Mitch didn't quite see it that way. Bruce had been fair with him, but he didn't feel that the older man had thought of him as a son in any way—even though for his part, he had regarded his boss as a second father.

"I think you just might have put the carriage before the horse," he told her.

She wasn't going to spend any more time arguing with Mitch about this.

"Whatever. Let's go see about that fence that needs fixing," she told him.

He was more than happy to oblige.

"I take it back," Mitch told her almost two hours later.

He and Ena had been working on the fence this entire time, taking down the sagging poles and replacing them, then nailing in new lengths of wood between the poles. It was going faster than he had anticipated. They were more than half-finished. He hadn't expected that, certainly not from her.

"Take what back?" Ena asked, taking a short break. She did a quick survey of her own work and was basically satisfied, although she noted that there were areas where she could have done a better job.

"You still have pretty hands, but you certainly know your way around fixing a fence," Mitch told her with a grin. "That shop teacher would certainly have been proud of you. Was it Mr. Pollard?" he asked, remembering the class he'd had with the man, except back then, Pollard had doubled as a football coach.

It had been years since she had thought about the potbellied shop teacher with the sagging trousers that he was forever hiking up. Envisioning him now, she recalled that he'd also had unruly yellow-white hair that looked like a haystack that was being blown around by a fierce wind.

Ena nodded in response to his question. "Yes, it was Mr. Pollard." More memories came back to her. "That man insisted on keeping us trapped in that room for the first half hour of each session while he regaled us with all these stories about the projects he'd made and how he always kept his students in line, no matter how unruly they tried to be."

Mitch was more than familiar with the man's shortcomings. "Well, he might have liked to hear himself talk, but he seemed to have done a good job teaching you how to work with wood."

She slanted a look in his direction. "Is that a compliment?"

"If you have to ask, I guess I wasn't being clear enough, but yes, that was a compliment. You did a really good job—and so did Mr. Pollard," Mitch added.

"Too bad your dad couldn't see this." He gestured toward the fence they were just working on. "He would have been really impressed."

But Ena wasn't buying any of it. "I really doubt that."

Mitch remained firm. "I don't."

Ena was silent for a long moment. And then she suddenly turned toward him. "Mitch?"

There was a different look in her eyes that caught his attention immediately. "Yes?"

"Where's he buried? My dad," she added in case he thought she was asking about Mr. Pollard or someone else for some reason.

Ena didn't know if her father had been buried, or if he'd been cremated and his ashes scattered somewhere. It hadn't even occurred to her—until just now.

"In the farthest corner of the cemetery," Mitch told her. "Just behind the church."

"The church?" she repeated in surprise. "My father never stepped one foot into a church in his entire life. Not even when my mother died." She recalled that awful day. It had rained appropriately enough. Nothing else had been appropriate about that pain-filled day. "He had her buried on the ranch."

"Your father changed his mind about that," he said, watching the surprised look on her face. "He had her casket exhumed and transferred to the cemetery. Miss Joan actually talked him into doing that," he explained. "She told him that your mother would be more at peace there. Shortly after that, your father made it known that he wanted to be buried next to his wife when his time finally came."

"So that's where he's buried? In the church cemetery?" Ena asked in surprise. That didn't sound like her father, she thought.

"Yup. Right alongside your mother. The whole town turned out for the funeral," he added.

"Did you pay them?" she asked, surprised by Mitch's statement. She couldn't recall her father *ever* having any friends. Why would anyone attend the funeral of a man they hardly knew?

Mitch almost laughed at her question but managed to catch himself just in time.

"No, but I think Miss Joan threatened a few people into going. Nobody says no to that lady. Not if they ever want to be able to eat at her diner again."

Ena nodded her head. That made more sense, she thought.

Chapter Nine

"Would you like me to take you?" Mitch offered when Ena had made no further comment about her father's burial plot.

Did he think she was a helpless female incapable of finding her way around? She wasn't sure if she should be insulted or if this was Mitch's attempt at being chivalrous.

"I grew up here, Parnell. For the most part I know every inch of this postage stamp–sized town. I can certainly take myself over to the cemetery—*if* I wanted to go."

"I didn't mean to imply that you couldn't. I just thought you might like some company."

Ena looked at him. That wasn't what he meant, she thought. "You mean moral support, don't you?" she corrected him.

But Mitch stuck to his guns. "No, I mean *company*

but if that's the way you want to see it," he went on ami-
cably, "then I'm not going to argue with you."

"No?" she questioned, annoyed. "I thought you liked
arguing."

"Not even remotely," Mitch replied. When she still
didn't answer his initial offer to accompany her to the
cemetery, he decided to prod her a little more. "So?"

Right now, Ena found that she couldn't deal with the
thought of looking down at the ground that was covering the loud, angry man who had once been her father. So instead of giving Mitch an answer one way or
another, she waved at the partially completed section
of the fence and said, "Let's just finish this, okay?"

Mitch inclined his head, acquiescing. "You're the
boss."

For a moment, that gave Ena pause as she rolled the
foreman's words over in her head.

"Yes," she finally agreed, brightening at his response. "I am."

Although, if she were being truthful with herself,
it was hard for her to think of herself in those terms.
Her father had been the boss on the Double E. With his
death, all that there was left behind was a vacuum, not
a place for her to take over and fill.

Logically, Ena knew she should aspire to that title,
but it honestly held no allure for her. She felt the same
way about becoming the boss at the accounting firm
where she worked. She had drive and ambition, but having others bow and scrape before her didn't interest her
in the slightest. She had always been far more interested
in doing the work than in pontificating to those who
were working for her.

However, for argument's sake, she agreed with
Mitch's pronouncement that she was the boss. In her

estimation it was the fastest way to get things moving along—and that, in her estimation, was all that really counted.

"Are you tired?" Mitch asked out of the blue after they had been at repairing the fence for close to another full hour.

"No," Ena answered a bit too quickly and, she realized, a bit too defensively. "Why?"

"No real reason." It was a lie actually, Mitch thought. He decided to be honest with her. "You just seemed to have slowed down, that's all."

It wasn't that she was tired. She'd slowed down because she felt that as soon as they finished repairing the fence, Mitch would ask her again if she wanted to visit her father's grave. She really didn't want to have that discussion. Didn't want Mitch thinking that she was afraid to go see the grave for some reason.

It wasn't fear that was keeping her from going. It was dealing with the idea of seeing both her parents in the ground while she was still alive and well, doing her best to come to grips with the whole scenario in which she was now all alone in the world.

"You're imagining things," she told Mitch dismissively.

Again he gave her no argument. "Maybe I am. Maybe I'm tired, too."

He was humoring her, saying that he was tired for her benefit, she thought. Under normal circumstances, she might have very well called him out on the lie. But in her present state of mind, she didn't want to get into it. It was better this way.

She was about to say that she felt like working longer, but he seemed to have anticipated that, as well.

"Hey, what do you say we call it quits for now and hang up our tools for the day?" Mitch's tone sounded pretty final.

Ena decided to take him up on his suggestion. The truth was she had pushed herself a bit too much just to prove that she could handle the work and now she was regretting it. Or at least her arms and shoulders were. She was really going to be sore tomorrow.

"Fine with me," she answered, trying to sound nonchalant. "Do you want to go back to the stable?"

"Eventually," he told her, putting the tools into the truck's flatbed.

Eventually. Okay, here it came. The last thing she needed was to have him lecture her about paying her "respects" to her father and that she would feel better once she made herself deal with that. Mentally, she dug in, waiting for Mitch to fire the first shot. She deliberately ignored the fact that being near him like this raised her body temperature and caused her heart to beat faster than it was supposed to. She tried to tell herself that she was utterly oblivious to him and the effect he had on her—but deep down inside her soul, she knew she was lying.

"And what is it that you intend on doing now?" she asked, spoiling for a fight and hoping that would get her mind off the rest of it.

Finished with the tools, he opened the driver's-side door. "I thought I'd swing by town, pick up some more supplies. We're running short on a few things."

"And that's it?" she questioned, stunned and disappointed, as well. "You're going shopping?"

"Yes, unless you have something else you want to do instead," he answered her innocently, knowing he was goading her. He loved seeing the fire enter her eyes.

Someday soon, he promised himself, that fire would be meant for him—and in a good way.

"Let me get this straight. You want to go into town to pick up some supplies," she repeated incredulously.

"That's what I said, yes," he told her, keeping a straight face.

"That sounds like an errand," she protested. "Don't you have someone you could tell to do that for you?"

"I could," Mitch agreed. "But I like looking around the general store for myself, in case there's something I forgot to put on the list. Besides," he said honestly, "I like mingling with people. It allows me to stay in touch with what's going on in town."

"So this isn't your way of getting me to swing by the church cemetery?"

"You made it sound like you didn't want to, so why should I do that?" he asked her.

Her eyes narrowed. "You're playing mind games with me."

"I think you're overthinking this and giving me way too much credit. I don't have time for mind games. I've got a ranch to run—for you," he added pointedly. "Now, if you like, I can bring you back to the stable or the ranch house," he added, "before I go into town for those supplies."

He was good at playing the innocent man, she'd give him that, Ena thought. She debated which way to play this for a moment, then made up her mind. This could work out after all.

"No, that's all right. I'll come into town with you. It might not be such a bad idea to look around for a bit," she told him.

He wasn't about to get sucked into a discussion over

this. "Whatever you say. Like I said before, you're the boss."

If that was true, she thought, slanting a glance in his direction, why did she have this feeling that she'd somehow been played?

Maybe Mitch was right. Maybe she was guilty of overthinking everything. Even so, she couldn't shake the feeling that the man was somehow very subtly manipulating her.

Lost in thought, she really hadn't done very much by way of helping him to secure the tools into the back of the truck. They went to stock up on supplies. Since Mitch was driving the pickup, it gave Ena a real opportunity to look around as they approached town.

Nothing had really changed in Forever, she thought. Oh, there were some new additions and perhaps there was a slightly busier air about the small town than there had been ten years ago. But for the most part, it still felt like the tiny town that half the more mournful country songs were written about. The kind of town it was good to be *from* but definitely not one to be living in at the present time.

She was just asking herself what she was doing back here when Mitch pulled up to an open spot right in front of the general store. The engine made a stuttering sound as he turned it off.

She could feel his eyes on her. When she turned toward him, he said, "You don't have to come in if you don't want to."

Was he trying to tell her something? Her years in the business world had made her suspicious of everything, unable to take *anything* at face value.

"Why wouldn't I want to?" she asked him.

"I was only thinking that you might not want to have

to put up with a whole bunch of questions fired at you. You remember what people are like in Forever," Mitch reminded her. "Always full of questions because nothing much goes on in their lives without gossip. They'd want to know if you were going to stay on now that you're back—and they'd probably ask you why you took off the way you did. They might even—"

Ena shut her eyes as she put up her hands to block the onslaught of words. "Stop. You've made your point. You might have thought of this earlier," she told the man in the front seat next to her.

His expression was easygoing and totally devoid of guilt. "You're right. Sorry," he apologized.

"Well, we're here now," she said with a sigh. "You talked me into it. I'll just stay in the truck," she decided.

Maybe he should have been more forceful about taking her back to the ranch house, Mitch thought. "I'll hurry," he promised.

Ena shifted in her seat. The truck's seat was definitely not made with comfort in mind. "You do that," she told him.

So much for reverse psychology, he thought as he walked quickly to the general store. He'd thought if he'd told her what she would be facing coming into the general store with him, Ena would have come with him just to prove that she could put up with a shower of questions and emerge unscathed.

Maybe he should have just let her get out of the truck and come with him without saying anything to encourage her to hang back. He had been certain that her desire to be the one in control would have had her coming into the store with him.

Well, he'd gambled and lost. No big deal, he told himself. Now all he could do was just hurry down the shopping list he'd brought with him and hope that Ena wasn't going to be in an irritated mood when he got back with the supplies.

"You in a hurry, Mitch?" Wallace Page asked.

The owner of the only store of this kind in Forever, Wallace, watched the foreman from the Double E Ranch move through the store, grabbing items and piling them all up on the counter. He didn't recall ever seeing Mitch move around so fast.

"You might say that," Mitch answered, depositing another large item on the counter, then heading back to the shelves for a sack of something else. "I've got someone waiting in the truck."

"Oh, so it's that way, is it?" Wallace said with a knowing laugh.

"No," Mitch denied patiently as he went to fetch another item on his list. "It's not any way, Wallace." Done, he quickly surveyed everything he'd picked up. "Just total all this up for me, please."

"Sure thing." The man's fingers flew over his almost ancient cash register keys, an item he had inherited from his father. "Need help getting these things to your truck?"

"All I need is to use the wagon to get it all out there," he told the owner.

"You want me to put it on the Double E's account?" the storeowner asked once he had finished totaling it all up.

"Like you always do, Wallace," Mitch responded.

"Hey, is that the O'Rourkes' girl with you?" Wallace suddenly asked. He craned his neck, trying to get a glimpse of the interior of Mitch's truck from his vantage point through the store's front window. The man's thin, pinched face fell. "Guess not," the man said, disappointed.

Mitch turned to look toward his truck. He was surprised to see that the passenger seat was empty. They were too far from the ranch for Ena to suddenly decide that she was going to walk home.

So where had she taken off to? When he'd left her, he hadn't gotten the impression that she wanted to go see anyone.

"I thought you said you had someone waiting for you in the truck," Wallace said, confused.

Still not willing to identify who he had brought with him, Mitch shrugged. "Guess they got tired of sitting around and waiting and decided to take in the local color."

Wallace cackled. "That's a good one, son. We all know that Forever doesn't have any local color," the general store owner declared with a shake of his head. "But maybe someday…"

"Yeah, maybe someday," Mitch agreed absently, hardly hearing what Wallace had said. "I'll see you next week, Wallace," he said.

Trying not to appear as if he were in a hurry—or worried—Mitch quickly unloaded the various boxes and sacks in the giant-sized wagon, then pushed the cart over toward where the other carts were lined up.

He debated driving around to look for Ena, but he didn't want to move his truck in case she had just gone for a walk and was returning to the vehicle. The idea of a walk, however, was highly doubtful.

"Where are you?" Mitch murmured under his breath, scanning the immediate area.

He thought of going to the diner, but if Ena *hadn't* gone there, Miss Joan would somehow intuit that there was something wrong and launch into her own version of the third degree. He didn't want to have to go through that unless it was absolutely necessary and he had no other recourse.

Standing there, looking up and down the streets of Forever, Mitch studied the various buildings in the area, thinking.

And then it occurred to him where Ena must have gone.

Still leaving the truck parked in front of the general store, he quickly hurried past the medical clinic and Murphy's, as well as a few other familiar places, until he reached the church.

Instead of going inside the recently renovated building, he went around it until he came to the back end of it.

The cemetery was located a small distance way.

Mitch walked quickly toward it. At first, it appeared that there was no one inside the gated area. And then, as he came closer, still scanning the area, he saw her.

Ena.

Mitch quickly lengthened his stride until he was inside the gated area.

For a moment, he debated whether or not he should withdraw and leave her alone before she saw him. He knew that she had to have gone through some rather deep soul-searching before she had talked herself into coming over here.

But he did want to be there for her in case Ena suddenly felt she needed him.

Looking around, he found a large tombstone that, if he stood just right, would block him from her sight. So he stood off to the side, observing her. Watching for some sort of sign that she suddenly desired him to be there for her, or to talk to. Whatever it took, Mitch wanted to be ready. He knew what it felt like to suddenly find himself all alone, the way she did now with her father's passing.

Being very careful to be as quiet as he could, Mitch realized that she was talking to the small headstone he had put up.

"Still calling the shots, aren't you, Dad?" Ena was saying to the headstone that had her father's name on it. "I see you moved Mom. At least you picked a better place for her this time than you did the last time. She never did like that old oak tree, you know, not that you cared about something like that.

"I guess this means that Mom's going to have to listen to you talk for all eternity." Ena shook her head. "That's not fair, you know. The poor woman earned her rest after having to put up with you for all those years. But then, you were never all that interested in what was fair, were you?"

Ena fell silent for a moment, searching for words. "I want you to know that you lucked out. That guy you took under your wing, the one you probably wished was your kid instead of me, well, he turned out to be a good man. He's running the place and doing a really good job. You would have been very proud." She pressed her lips together. "Maybe you should have left the ranch to him. He certainly earned it. But then, you probably never made him feel the way you made me feel."

"He regretted that, you know."

Startled because she was so engrossed in talking to the spirit of her father, she hadn't realized that someone was there, listening to her.

Ena turned around to find herself looking up at Mitch.

Chapter Ten

Ena's defenses instantly went up. How long had the man been standing there, listening to her "talk" to her dead father?

Annoyed and embarrassed, she could feel her cheeks growing hot.

Her eyes blazed as she looked at him. "Are you spying on me?" she demanded.

"No, I went out looking for you," he explained calmly. "When I came out to the truck with the supplies, you weren't sitting in the cab. You'd told me that you were going to wait in the truck until I got back, so when I didn't see you, I got concerned."

She supposed that if she weren't so embarrassed because Mitch had overheard her "talking" to her father, she might have found his concern to be almost touching. But she *was* embarrassed, and right now, she just wanted to move past this whole incident and forget that it had ever taken place.

"There was no reason for you to be worried," she told him gruffly. "It's not like I could have been kidnapped by some drug lord or something. This is Forever, for heaven's sake. *Nothing* ever happens in Forever," she maintained flatly.

"I wouldn't be so sure if I were you," he told her. "Things happen here." He saw the skeptical look on her face and pressed on, "*Life* happens here. The sheriff met his wife here because Olivia came searching for her sister when Tina ran off with the father of her baby. Everyone wound up here," he told her.

"Well, they weren't from around here originally," Ena stressed, as if that made her point.

"Yes, but they live here now. At least Olivia and Tina do, along with Tina's baby. And it might interest you to know that Tina is now married to one of the town's doctors—Dr. Davenport, who also came from the Northeast. New York City to be specific. And theirs isn't the only story like that.

"My point," Mitch continued, "is that we don't live in some kind of bubble here. People from all over the country come through here, and when they do, they bring life with them. And they *choose* to stay here."

Ena closed her eyes and sighed, giving up. "Okay, you made your point. But nothing dramatic happened to me," she informed him. Then, to explain why she'd left the truck, she said, "You talked about my father and my mother being buried in the church cemetery and I thought that I'd just come take a look at their headstones for myself. Mystery solved."

Her expression was almost stony, he thought, trying to guess what was going on in her head.

"And now that you did?" Mitch asked. When she

didn't say anything in response, he tried to prod her a little. "Any thoughts?"

Ena glanced back at the two tombstones that marked her parents' graves.

"Yes," she said grudgingly. "You picked out nice headstones."

"Actually," he told her, "your father picked those out. Since he knew he was dying, he wanted to tie up all the loose ends that he could while he was still able to get around. He went to that mortuary in the next town and made all the arrangements. Your dad was a very determined man. He kept on working until he was too weak to get out of bed."

Try as she might to block out the wave of intense guilt that had suddenly risen up, it managed to break through, drenching her. She hated feeling this way and attempted to deflect her guilt by blaming the man next to her.

"You should have found a way to locate me and let me know that my father was dying." There was unmistakable hostility in Ena's voice.

His answer was the same as Miss Joan's had been. But it was prefaced with a twist she hadn't expected. "He already knew where you were but he didn't want to disrupt your life."

Ena stared at Mitch, stunned. "Wait, he *knew* where I was?" That wasn't possible, she thought. She had moved twice since the last Christmas card she'd sent to her father years ago.

Mitch hesitated. He was telling tales out of school, but he supposed at this point, what did it matter? She needed to know that her father *did* care about her despite whatever she thought she knew.

"Your father had a private investigator track you down," he told her.

That just confused things further for her. "I don't understand. If he went to such great lengths to have me found, why didn't he come to see me?"

That was simple enough to answer. "He went to such great lengths because he wanted to make sure you were still all right. The private investigator he'd hired told him that you had put yourself through college and that after graduation, you'd found an accounting position with a good, reputable firm.

"The private investigator assured your father that you were doing well. But you know your dad, he wasn't just going to accept the man's word for that so the investigator produced pictures as well as written evidence to back up what he was saying. It was all included in the report he wrote up for your father. I can show it to you if you'd like," Mitch offered.

It still didn't make any sense to her. "But if he had all that information, if he knew where I was, why didn't he even *try* to come see me?"

"My guess is that your father was a proud man. His feeling was that you left him. He didn't leave you. He undoubtedly thought that the ball was in your court—meaning that it was up to you to come back."

She could see that under normal circumstances, but not in the end. "But when he knew he was dying, he could have gotten word to me—"

"Again, he was a proud man," Mitch repeated. "He didn't want pity to be the motivating reason you came back."

Ena shook her head, frustrated. She glared at the headstone. "The man's dead and he's still making me crazy."

"I guess that was his gift," Mitch told her with a quiet smile.

She wouldn't have called it a gift. "How did you put up with him?" Ena asked.

"Oh, he had his good points." Mitch looked at the headstone and thought of the man buried there. "He treated me fairly, gave me a roof over my head, became like a second father to me. A stern father," he granted, "but to a kid without anyone, that was a lot."

For a moment, she felt a little jealous of the relationship between her father and the foreman. A relationship she would have given anything to have. "I guess he was lucky to have you."

"That went both ways," Mitch told her. And then he added contritely, "Look, I'm sorry I intruded on your time here. Why don't I go back to the truck and wait for you there? Take all the time you want, then come find me when you're done. The truck's still parked in front of the general store."

Now that Mitch had walked in on her, Ena felt awkward about spending any more time there. Anyway, she had basically said everything she had wanted to say to her father.

"I'm done," she announced.

Mitch looked at her uncertainly. "Are you sure?"

Ena shrugged. "There's just so much a person can say to a headstone," she answered glibly.

"Your mother was there, too," Mitch gently pointed out.

"I don't need to look at a piece of stone to talk to my mother. I talk to her in my heart," she informed him. Turning, she began to walk toward the cemetery exit. "Didn't you say you loaded up the truck with supplies?" she asked.

"I did."

"Well," she said impatiently, "isn't there something in those supplies that's melting or rotting or coming apart by now?"

"No, but I get the message," he told Ena, the corners of his mouth curving ever so slightly. "You want to go back to the ranch."

That was putting it rather bluntly, but there was no denying that he was right. "Very good. What gave me away?" she asked him sardonically.

"I guess it was just my steel-trap mind," he responded. "I also have the ability to read minds on occasion, so if I were you, I'd stick to thinking pure thoughts."

She laughed at that, her mood mercifully lightened. "I suppose that means I can't fantasize about strangling you?"

"Not at the moment," he answered, then grinned. "But maybe later."

Bemused, she shook her head. "You are one very weird man."

He flashed another grin at her, and although she tried not to let it get to her, she couldn't deny that it did.

"I'll take that as a compliment."

Ena frowned at him, but her heart really wasn't in it. "I'm not sure that I meant it as one."

"That's okay," he told her, enjoying himself. "I can still take it as one."

The ride back to the ranch was less awkward than the one she had experienced coming into the town. It was as if, because of the things that Mitch had shared with her, an unspoken truce had been struck up between them.

In addition, Ena no longer felt that Mitch had some

sort of hidden agenda when it came to her or to running the ranch. She'd decided that Mitch was on the level and that he just wanted to live up to the promise he had made to her father.

Ena glanced at Mitch's chiseled profile. For a moment, she had to admit to herself that she was glad that he had been there in her father's last days.

I guess you really did find the son you always wanted, Dad. Sorry it couldn't have been me, she thought as they approached the ranch house.

Even in her present mind-set, it still took Ena several days before she worked up the courage to finally walk into her father's room.

In part it was because she didn't want to deal with any unanticipated painful old memories. Being in her father's house was difficult enough for her. Entering the man's room, his "inner sanctum" so to speak, was another matter entirely. In addition, she didn't want to accidentally stumble across anything that might make those old memories even worse.

Mitch hadn't said anything about it, but maybe her father had taken up with someone in the last years of his life. Someone who had replaced her mother in his eyes.

Ena wasn't certain how she would deal with that.

Yes, her father had had every right to see someone. After all, he had been a widower and he had also been a grown man who needed companionship.

But after the surly way he had been toward her mother, there was a part of Ena that felt her father had no right to look for and find that sort of happiness with someone else.

So she wavered about walking into his room. Eventually, she lost her temper with herself. This was stupid.

She was a grown woman. She could handle whatever she might find—not to mention that there might be nothing to find.

With effort, Ena managed to steel herself, blocking out any extraneous thoughts that could get in her way and torpedo what she was attempting to do. She was strictly on a fact-finding mission, she told herself. She wanted to get a sense of how her father had spent the last ten years of his life, and while asking Mitch questions would certainly help fill in the gaps, Mitch might have his own agenda when it came to dealing with this. He might be trying to keep things from her because, for whatever reason of his own making, he wanted her to think well of her father.

Too late for that, she thought, although she had to admit that some of her thoughts had been tempered and softened a bit because of the things that Mitch had told her.

Still, she didn't want the foreman to influence the way she ultimately viewed her father's last days. All she had to do was summon eighteen years of bad memories and any good things that Mitch might have had to say were in serious jeopardy.

The second she finally walked into her father's bedroom, a sense of his presence instantly seeped under her skin. He'd been dead for a month and she could swear she could still smell the soap he always used.

She slowly looked around the exceptionally masculine room.

"Well, I'm here, Old Man. You got your way. At least for now," she qualified. "You got any hidden surprises to spring on me? Something to make me feel that I wasn't a total fool for coming here?" Ena walked around the room, touching things. Thinking. "Because if you think that the ranch is my consolation prize for enduring everything that went down between us, you're wrong. I don't want the ranch. I *never* wanted the ranch. That was always your thing," she said, addressing the air with a touch of bitterness in her voice.

"I'm planning on selling the ranch the first chance I get once the deed is officially in my name. So I'm going to put up with those conditions you stuck into the will. I'm going to live up to my end of it, and you, you're going to live up to yours. Pardon my pun," she told her father's spirit whimsically.

Roaming around the darkly furnished room, she thought of how he had removed all traces of her mother from what had once been their bedroom. Even the curtains that she had put up were gone. Her father had hung drapes in their place.

Opening his closet showed her that he had taken all her mother's clothing and put them away, as well. Most likely *gave* them away.

But there was no evidence that her father had taken up with another woman. There was no trace of anyone else in the room. No clothing, no small bottles of perfume left behind and forgotten. Not so much as an empty makeup container.

Still, she was her father's daughter, which made her inherently want to be completely thorough. So she moved around the room, opening doors and drawers, rummaging through any and all places, trying to find something that didn't belong.

Ena was very nearly finished with her search when she found it.

A rectangular box shoved all the way into the recesses of her father's closet.

The lid on the box was secured by several large

rubber bands the size of small bungee cords. The fact that it had so many cords aroused her curiosity.

Moving very carefully, she took off one cord after another until she could finally lift the lid off unimpeded.

This had to be it, Ena thought. Whatever was inside here probably had to do with her father's mystery lady. The person he had at least hoped to replace her mother with.

Ena sat down on the edge of the bed with the box next to her. Taking a deep breath, she braced herself, then slowly lifted the lid.

There were several envelopes in the box, all addressed to her father.

Recognition was immediate.

The handwriting was hers.

The envelopes had been from her, sent to her father those first two Christmases so that he wouldn't worry that something had happened to her. She'd been so sure that he had thrown them away. He certainly hadn't acknowledged them.

She could remember waiting each year, long past Christmas, for some word from him, but there hadn't been any.

Her hands trembled a little as she took out the first card. The note she had written to her father fell out. When she picked it up, she could see that the paper was worn, like it had been taken out and read over and over again, then carefully returned to its envelope.

She took out the last one. This note looked like the first note had: worn from frequent handling. The notes hadn't been crumpled in anger or torn the way she would have expected. Just worn because they'd been read and reread countless times.

By a man who would have loudly protested that he didn't care—but obviously had.

She sighed, holding the letters in her hand. Her eyes stung and she blinked, determined not to shed a single tear.

But she ultimately lost that battle the way she knew she would.

Chapter Eleven

It was turning into one big perpetual juggling act.

Because Ena didn't want to run the risk of possibly losing her position in the hierarchy at the firm where she had worked so hard to get ahead, three days a week Ena got up before the crack of dawn to work on the accounts that had been forwarded to her via email. She took them on because she had always believed in shouldering her responsibilities, not shirking them, and these were her accounts.

But as the days went by, she began to feel that her heart wasn't in this as much as it had been. While there was a certain satisfaction working with numbers, it wasn't the same sort of satisfied feeling she derived from working with the horses.

Besides, she discovered around the latter half of the second week she was there, if she were really looking to balance a ledger, she had her father's accounts to work with.

Or, more to the point, to set right.

"You really didn't have a head for figures, did you, Old Man?" she marveled, addressing the hodgepodge that Bruce O'Rourke had undoubtedly referred to as his accounting method.

As Ena paged through the worn ledger that looked as if it had been used as a doorstop more than once, she was stunned to see that her father had left some columns completely blank and others without any totals whatsoever. Toward the latter half of the book, there was hardly a balanced statement to be found.

Piecing things together, Ena concluded that her father had stopped keeping records, or at least accurate records, somewhere around the time that her mother had taken ill. And it had all gone downhill from there.

Prior to that, the columns had all been neatly written. She looked closer and saw that every number was written in her mother's very precise handwriting.

"She was your accountant, wasn't she, Old Man?" Ena murmured.

She frowned, flipping through the pages. It looked as if not only wasn't her father's heart in the work but he had barely paid attention to it, and when he did, it all looked as if it was haphazard and slipshod.

Getting this in order was going to take a monumental effort, she thought.

"There you are," Mitch declared as he came into the den. "I was looking for you. Felicity said you had breakfast early. Are you ready to get to work?" he asked.

She spared him a quick glance. "I *am* working," she informed him. "Did you know that my father's records were a complete mess?"

Mitch shook his head, although her question didn't

surprise him. "He never let me look at any of that. Always said that he had it all under control."

She frowned as she turned another page, all but shuddering at what she found. This was going to take her weeks and weeks to straighten out, if not longer, she thought in mounting despair.

"Well, he lied," she told the foreman.

"Maybe he didn't realize how bad this was," Mitch guessed.

That, she thought, was being far too kind. "Oh, I think he knew exactly how bad this was. He probably didn't care. To him, ledgers and accounts weren't what ranching was about. That kind of thing was just a nuisance that he felt just got in his way." She thought back to her childhood. "As long as he made enough money selling horses to pay his men and to keep the ranch afloat, he figured he was doing all right."

"But he wasn't?" Mitch asked, waiting for her to fill in the details.

Ena flipped to another page. It was just as awful as its predecessors. Closer examination showed her that there were entries on those pages without any sort of rhyme or reason.

She sighed. "So far from all right that I don't see how it didn't catch up to him long ago."

"Does this mean you're going to lose the ranch?" Mitch asked. It was obvious that he was concerned.

Ena shook her head. "Not if I can help it. It's going to take some clever calculating and manipulation of figures, but I think that the situation might be salvageable."

"Well, if anyone can do it, you can," Mitch said with confidence.

Ena blinked. Now he was just trying to butter her

up. "How can you say that? You don't know anything about my work."

"No," Mitch agreed. "But I do know you," he pointed out. He paused for a second, debating whether or not to say the next words. He decided he had nothing to lose. "Knew the kind of person you were all the way back in high school. You're not someone who just gives up. You dig in and fight for what you want."

She looked at him, surprised by what he had said. "All those years back in high school, I thought you didn't even know I existed. Other than just to nod at." And that had only been when she nodded first.

His smile widened as he looked at her. "Oh, I knew. And I paid attention."

She thought back to the way she had tried to get his attention. No matter what she had done, he had just ignored her. Or at least that was the way it had seemed.

"Then why—"

"Didn't I ever ask you out?" Mitch guessed at the rest of her question. "Because I felt that you were out of my league and I didn't want you to shoot me down when you figured that out. I had a very fragile ego back then. Put that together with being the *new kid* as well as being in the foster system, and I just didn't have enough courage to ask you out and risk ultimately getting turned down. Besides, I knew who your father was and, to be honest, I was pinning all my hopes on getting a job on his ranch when I graduated."

She hadn't realized that. She just thought it was a coincidence that he had wound up working here. "So, in a way, this was because of my father?" she asked incredulously.

He couldn't very well say no after he'd told her the first part. "In a very roundabout way," Mitch allowed.

"For the most part, it was because you were such a big deal and I didn't have the nerve to fall flat on my face—so I never asked you out."

"Huh," she said, turning the swivel chair around to face him squarely. The chair squeaked as it turned, making her wince. "I wouldn't have pegged you for a coward," she told Mitch.

"I'm not—anymore," he told her. "And I've got your father to thank for that. He helped me build up my confidence, made me feel that I was capable of doing things."

Listening to him, Ena shook her head. "It still doesn't seem like we're talking about the same man. The Bruce O'Rourke I knew never built up anyone's self-esteem. As a matter of fact, the old man seemed to thrive on destroying self-esteem."

"Maybe your leaving was what changed him," Mitch told her. "Because according to some of the old-timers who were there when I started to work on the ranch, your dad had the kind of disposition that made rattle-snakes duck and hide."

Ena laughed despite herself. "Now *that* sounds like my dad," she told him.

He liked hearing her laugh. She looked good in a smile, he thought. It just brightened her whole face. "Like I said, he changed after you left. Because of that—and thanks to you—he became a fair boss. Stern, like I said, but really fair. And I found that I could always talk to him."

She was really having trouble making her peace with what Mitch was telling her.

"Well, that made one of us, because I certainly never could, not even when my mother was alive. After she died, life with my father became just like doing time in hell."

There was sympathy in his eyes as he looked at her. "Was he that bad?"

"He was actually worse, but I don't use that kind of language, so my description of hell is going to have to do," Ena told him.

Mitch came around the desk, and to Ena's surprise, he took her hand, coaxing her up out of the chair. "Why don't you leave all that for now?"

"But it's been in this state for *years* now," she complained.

"That's my whole point," Mitch told her. "If it's been that way for all this time, it can certainly last for another day. No need to kill yourself to try to get it fixed as fast as you can. As a matter of fact," he said, considering the ordeal she was determined to take on, "tackling this behemoth in stages might be a better way to go if you think about it. This way, you won't wind up completely wiped out."

"Stages, eh?" she asked and Mitch nodded in response. "You, Parnell, have a very unique approach to working," Ena told him.

"It's called prioritizing, and it seems to have worked out for me so far so I feel like I can honestly recommend it to you." His voice grew serious. "There's nothing to be gained by working yourself into the ground like that. If you're *not* wiped out, you can come back and work on this another day. So, how about it?" he asked. "You know the foal's been asking for you."

"Right," she said with a laugh. "And did he *ask* for me by name?"

Mitch winked at her as he said, "Well, as a matter of fact..."

The man was incredible, Ena thought, amused. "Well,

if we're dealing with a talking foal, let's not keep him waiting," she responded. "Let's go pay the little guy a visit."

"Now that's the ticket," Mitch encouraged. Then, without thinking, he put his arm around her shoulders and guided her out of the den and toward the front door as if they were old friends.

Ena felt something warm sparking within her chest and moving through her limbs. For now she decided to just enjoy it without analyzing it any further.

She was spreading herself thin and she knew it, Ena thought. But unlike what Mitch had suggested, she couldn't seem to get herself to prioritize the various duties that faced her.

There was doing the daily work on the ranch—something she knew Mitch and the hands who were working here could have taken on themselves, but that wasn't the point, according to the terms of her father's will. She was here to do the work, not shirk it.

There was also the huge mess that was otherwise known as her father's accounts. They were *so* jumbled up she knew it was going to take her *days*, if not longer, to untangle and straighten out. And then, of course, there were the accounts that were being emailed to her from Dallas. Accounts that she had insisted she could work on while away from the office.

Maybe she had taken on more than she was equipped to handle, Ena thought, staring at her father's ledger. After all, she wasn't exactly some sort of superheroine. She knew that.

But her pride wouldn't allow her to let anything she had taken on slide. So she found a way to spend time on all of it. The days were for the ranch, the early mornings and late evenings were for the accounts she had told her firm she would look into. And the four and a half minutes that were leftover were for her father's all but hopeless accounts.

That was what she was working on now, sitting in the den at her father's old scarred desk, struggling to keep her eyes from closing and desperately trying to figure out an old entry she had come across.

It made less than no sense to her.

Ena sighed, massaging the bridge of her nose, trying to keep at bay a possible headache that was forming right between her eyes.

"Whatever made you think you could tackle math, Old Man?" she murmured, looking at the page she had open. "This would have made more sense if you'd let your horse handle the accounts."

"You do realize that you need to get some sleep, right?"

Startled, she looked up. Mitch had come into the room. She hadn't even heard him walk in. But then, she was getting used to that.

"What I need is to understand why my father thought he could handle the books and why in heaven's name he didn't just get someone to do it for him," she said with a sigh. She fought a strong urge to toss the ledger across the room—or out the window.

"Could be that he was as stubborn as you are," Mitch speculated.

She didn't like being compared to her father. Ena raised her chin defensively. "At least I know my limits," she told him.

Mitch perched on the edge of the old desk, looking down at her. "Do you?" he asked, amused.

Her eyes narrowed as she pinned him with a look. "Just what is it that you are insinuating, Parnell?" she asked.

"Not insinuating," he responded. "I'm stating it blatantly. You're trying to do too much and you're looking to get yourself sick."

Ena could feel her temper rising. "Not my intention," she retorted.

"Maybe not," Mitch allowed. "But that's the end result. You're trying to juggle too many things at once, and eventually, one of those things is going to fall and hit you right in the head."

"Colorful," she commented cryptically.

"Also true," Mitch insisted. "Call it a day and go to bed," he advised.

She felt really punchy at this point and it was making her cranky. "You're not in charge of me, Parnell."

"No, you're right, I'm not. But that doesn't mean that I want to stand by and watch you get sick—and if you keep on going like this, trying to do two and a half jobs, you just might. Your dad wanted you to work the ranch. He didn't mean that you should go on doing your other job and also cleaning up his account books at the same time. I'm fairly sure of that," Mitch added with just the slightest touch of sarcasm.

That only served to make Ena angrier. "That's because he didn't think I could do anything," Ena said, remembering the way her father used to regard her.

"So now, by knocking yourself out this way, you're going to *show* him, is that it?" Mitch asked.

"Of course not," she snapped. When he continued to look at her with that "knowing" expression on his face, she had to struggle to hold on to her temper. "I can't *show* him because he's dead."

"That's right, he is," Mitch agreed quietly, his eyes still on hers. "So killing yourself like this really serves no purpose."

"Other than fulfilling the terms of the will, allowing me to continue to hold on to my job in Dallas, not to mention not losing the ranch to a bunch of bill collectors my father somehow either forgot to pay or just hoped would go away," she said, her voice building with each word she said.

Mitch slid off the desk and came around to look over her shoulder at the ledger that was opened on the desk.

"Is it really that bad?" he asked her.

She felt hemmed in right now and scrubbed her hand over her face. "Well, it's definitely not good."

"Can you do anything about it?" Mitch couldn't help thinking of all the people he worked with—people who were counting on the ranch continuing to operate so they could earn a living.

Ena pressed her lips together as she looked at the ledger entries—the ones she could make sense out of. "Depends on whether I can talk some people into granting the ranch extensions until we can get everything under control." She shook her head, her eyes all but glazing over. "He really should have asked for help with all this."

"Not in his nature," Mitch told her. "You know that."

"Yes, if I know anything, I know that," she agreed. She leaned back against the chair, stretching her shoulders. Her eyes kept insisting on closing. "You're right. I should go to bed."

Finally! "Glad to hear that," Mitch said.

"Just as soon as I get up enough strength," she mumbled.

The next thing he knew, Ena had fallen asleep right in front of him, still sitting back in the chair.

Chapter Twelve

Mitch touched Ena's arm. She didn't react. She was sound asleep.

"Well, I guess strength isn't going to be coming any-time soon. Looks like you just completely ran out of energy," he observed, looking at Ena. And then he assessed the situation. "Well, you certainly can't sleep in this chair. If you do, everything's going to ache when you wake up in the morning. You won't be any good to anyone then, least of all yourself."

There was only one thing to do. He needed to get her into her bed.

As gently as possible, he slipped his arm under her legs. Getting a secure hold, he picked Ena up from the chair. She stirred and made a noise, but her eyes remained closed.

Mitch released the breath he was holding, and he started to walk slowly. Leaving the den, he headed for the stairs.

Ena stirred again. Mitch walked even slower, certain that she was going to wake up at any second. But instead, she curled up into him as if he were a living, breathing pillow.

You're really making this hard, Ena, Mitch thought, doing his best not to allow the warmth he felt emanating from her body to infiltrate his. But it wasn't easy, especially not when working so closely with her had brought back all his old feelings for her, all those carefully blocked-out desires.

It was harder now. He was no longer that awkward teen pining after someone he felt was out of his league. He had gained self-confidence since then and holding her in his arms like this just brought all those old sensations back to him.

Vividly.

"You really know how to get to a man," he murmured to her under his breath.

Careful to take the stairs slowly because the last thing he wanted was to wake Ena, he moved up the steps cautiously, watching her face as he did so.

Midway up the stairs she sighed and seemed to curl into him even more, nestling her face against his chest. All sorts of stirrings were dancing about in the pit of his stomach.

Funny, he thought, after all this time, she was still the only one who could make him feel this way. Not that he was all that experienced. He wasn't a womanizer by any means, but then he wasn't exactly a shrinking violet, either. There had been women in his life, women from both his late mother's world as well as his late father's. There had been a mixture of both cultures.

But there had never been *the* woman.

He had just assumed that he wasn't meant to feel that

wild, heady, intoxicating excitement that a man experienced when the right woman crossed his path.

And then, suddenly here she was, the woman who somehow could raise his body temperature just by *being*, and here he was, carrying her up to her room.

To put her to bed and then just slip away, he silently reminded himself.

Clay Washburn, his best friend back when he and Clay had barely been teens, would have just shaken his head in despair.

He hadn't thought about Clay in years. Not since the car accident had happened, the one that had robbed him of his teen confidante.

He thought of him now. Clay had been a ladies' man, able to completely charm any woman who crossed his path within moments of the occurrence.

But although he thought of Clay fondly, he had never aspired to be anything like that himself. Being a ladies' man just wasn't his style. It required too much work, too much planning and he had never even had a desire to win a woman over.

Not until now.

Don't go there, Mitch warned himself. *She is not here to be seduced by you. She's here so she can fulfill the terms of her father's will. She's not here to get to know you better.*

Why couldn't it be both? Mitch wondered suddenly. After all, there was no rule that said it couldn't be both.

He was tired. That was why his mind was straying like this. He'd definitely be able to think more clearly in the morning, he promised himself, carefully shouldering open Ena's bedroom door.

Still moving very slowly, Mitch stepped inside the room.

There was only a crescent moon out and it illuminated almost nothing. The bedroom was more or less totally in pitch-darkness.

Even though he'd left the door open when he walked in, Mitch made his way to the bed very carefully. He made sure to take incredibly small steps so he wouldn't trip over anything or bump into something that would ultimately jar Ena awake.

So he stood inside the doorway for a second, waiting for his eyes to adjust to the dark. He wanted to be able to make out shapes that were in the room.

Once his vision had adjusted, Mitch made the rest of his way toward the bed. Reaching it, he very carefully laid Ena on top of the comforter.

A small bereft sort of sound seemed to escape from her lips and he froze.

Mitch debated covering her, then decided that he had pressed his luck too much as it was. If he tried to put the comforter over her, Ena could very well wind up waking.

"See you in the morning," he told Ena softly as he began to retrace his steps and retreat from Ena's bedroom.

"If you're lucky."

Mitch stopped dead and then slowly turned around. Was he hearing things, or had she suddenly woken up and spoken to him?

He had his answer when he finally looked at her face. Ena's eyes were open and she was smiling directly at him.

"You're awake," he said needlessly.

Ena grinned, even though she really did look tired. "Looks that way, doesn't it?"

Crossing back to her, he had one question. "When did you wake up?"

She looked a wee bit guilty as she said, "Just when you started going up the stairs."

That didn't make any sense to him. She was so independent—why would she have allowed him to carry her into her room if she was awake? "Why didn't you say anything?"

"Because I was really, really tired and it felt really nice to be whisked off to my room like that. Besides, I was curious if you were going to try anything," she told him, growing very sleepy again. Ena sighed as she curled up on the bed. "Nice to know that you're a gentleman."

"Yeah," Mitch muttered. "Nice for one of us at least," he said under his breath.

She heard him, but she was really too tired to call him out on it.

Besides, there was time enough to do that in the morning. After she got her rest…

Ena was asleep before she could even finish her thought.

The following morning the full significance of what had transpired the night before hit her. Mitch Parnell was the rarest of birds, an actual gentleman. He'd brought her up to her room, and even though he had thought she was asleep, he hadn't attempted anything.

However, Ena couldn't help thinking it meant he wasn't remotely attracted to her. But even though it could be deemed as being self-centered on her part, she was fairly confident that he *was* attracted to her.

The thought made her smile.

Widely.

"Well, someone certainly looks happy this morning," Felicity commented when Ena walked into the kitchen.

"I just got a really good night's sleep," Ena told the housekeeper. The latter was standing by the stove, looking like she was about to spring into action at any moment.

Hearing what Ena had just said, the housekeeper nodded her salt-and-pepper head.

"It is about time." When Ena looked at her quizzically, the woman said, "I am not deaf. I hear you working and moving things around in your father's den. I know you are working two jobs."

"Three," Ena corrected her. "But who's counting?"

The housekeeper's lips curved just the slightest bit. "You seem to be," Felicity noted. "Otherwise you would not have corrected me."

"Fair enough," Ena allowed. She looked around again. "Where's Mitch?"

"Mr. Mitch has already had his breakfast," Felicity told her.

Ena hadn't expected that. "Why didn't he wake me up?" she asked.

"Because he didn't want to," Felicity said simply. "Mr. Mitch left strict orders not to wake you," the housekeeper said, anticipating Ena's next question. "But he also said to make sure you had breakfast when you did come down."

"Where is he this morning?" Ena asked the woman.

Felicity gave her a stern look, as if she knew that her late boss's daughter would dash out the moment she had that information. "Mr. Mitch said I could tell you only *after* you have had breakfast."

Ena's good mood was quickly evaporating. "Felicity, I'm not in the mood to play games."

"Good, because I am not playing games," the woman informed her. "I am listening to Mr. Mitch's instructions," Felicity declared with more than a touch of pride.

Ena's eyes narrowed. She made one final attempt to get the woman to give up the information.

"You do know that I'm the one who pays your salary," she reminded Felicity.

"What I know is that Mr. Mitch is concerned about you and what he said to me makes good sense." Felicity looked at her sternly. "Now, the sooner you eat your breakfast, the sooner I can tell you where to find Mr. Mitch and the other men. Now, then," she said, giving her a penetrating look, "what is it that you would like to have for breakfast?"

Ena sighed. She had a feeling that Felicity could go on like this all day until she surrendered—so she did. "Scrambled eggs."

The housekeeper nodded, looking pleased. "Very good. Toast?"

Ena shrugged. "Sure, why not?" she said. Then she specified, "One slice."

The housekeeper opened up the loaf of bread and deposited two slices into the toaster.

"Two is better," the woman said with a finality that told Ena the matter wasn't up for discussion. She was getting two slices and that was that. And then she asked, "Coffee? Orange juice?"

Ena wasn't in the mood for either, but that wasn't the way this game was played and she knew it, so she replied, "Whatever it takes for you to tell me where Parnell is."

The housekeeper smiled with satisfaction. "Coffee and orange juice it is," she declared, pleased that Ena had come around.

Moving quickly, it only took the woman less than five minutes to whip up the aforementioned breakfast and put it on a plate.

"You will chew this slowly," the housekeeper told Ena as she set the plate of scrambled eggs and toast down in front of her. She eyed Ena and told her, "Foxing food down is bad for you."

Caught off guard, Ena stared at the housekeeper for a long moment—and then a light suddenly went off in her head.

"You mean *wolfing*," Ena corrected the older woman.

Felicity shrugged indifferently. "Fox, wolf, they are both small sneaky animals that like to eat on the move," she said, eyeing Ena to get her point across. "You will eat what I have made sitting down and you will eat it slowly."

There was no mistaking that the housekeeper had just issued an order.

Resigned, Ena did as the woman specified.

She fought a very strong urge to ask the housekeeper if she wanted her to chew each bite a certain amount of times. With her luck, the woman would answer in the affirmative and then pull a high number out of the air, making sure she followed through.

So Ena sat at the table and dutifully ate her breakfast.

Felicity's voice droned on in the background, telling her something to the effect that she, Ena, was very lucky to have someone as thoughtful as *Mr. Mitch* looking after her.

And then Felicity dropped a bombshell.

"He looked after Mr. Bruce, too, when Mr. Bruce got sick," she told Ena proudly.

"He did?" she asked. This was the first she had heard about this. Mitch had never mentioned doing this.

Felicity nodded. "He did," she confirmed. "Looked after Mr. Bruce like a son. *Better* than a son," she corrected. "I was here, of course, doing what I could to help out, but Mr. Bruce was too proud to accept my help. It was Mr. Mitch who took care of him, who helped him get dressed in the morning and into bed at night. Mr. Mitch made Mr. Bruce feel that he—Mr. Bruce—was doing him a favor by allowing him to help. He is a very good man, Mr. Mitch," Felicity said with feeling.

"So I'm beginning to learn," Ena said quietly. Finished with breakfast, she placed her utensils in the middle of the plate and pushed the plate away into the center of the table. "All right, I've satisfied his conditions, *now* will you tell me where I can find Mitch and the other men?" she asked, looking at Felicity expectantly and waiting for the woman to live up to her end of the bargain.

The housekeeper volunteered the information as if it was only logical and Ena should have figured it out for herself.

"Mr. Mitch said that he and the other men would be breaking in the new horses."

"Does that mean that he's at the corral right now?" Ena asked.

"Not the one closer to the house," Felicity specified. "He uses the corral behind the second barn to break in the horses."

Ena didn't bother asking why the change in venue had been made. She just wanted to get out and find Mitch. Felicity's revelation just now had caused a host of questions to pop up in her head.

"Thank you," Ena said as she rose to her feet. After draining the last of her coffee, she put the cup down, then told the housekeeper, "The breakfast you served this morning was very good."

Felicity nodded, accepting the words as her due. "I know."

Ena smiled to herself as she left the kitchen. Felicity was in a class by herself. She couldn't help wondering if the older woman and her father had clashed. Most likely on a daily basis. But the woman spoke fondly of her father, so either she had a high tolerance for frustration, or, at bottom, Felicity and her father understood each other.

Better woman than me, Felicity, Ena thought.

Leaving the house, she stood outside for a moment, looking around and absorbing her surroundings.

It was a beautiful, crisp morning. A good morning to be alive, Ena thought. She had skipped working on the accounts that her firm had forwarded, as well as playing hooky from working on her father's hodgepodge of a ledger this morning. And if she were being totally honest with herself, she had to admit that ignoring both things felt good.

She also realized that she was actually looking forward to working with the horses today. She liked ranch work. She could get back to the grind of working on her father's ledger and the accounts later this evening, but right now, she was eager to find Mitch. For a number of reasons.

Chapter Thirteen

If Ena hadn't already known where she was going, the sound of raised, cheering male voices would have guided her to the right destination. Mitch had told her yesterday that the focus today was going to be breaking in some of the newer horses. He'd even mentioned that the process on some of the horses had already been started.

What she hadn't expected—but looking back, Ena realized that she should have—was that the man who was doing the breaking was Mitch.

Her breath caught in her throat as she came closer to the corral and saw what Mitch was doing. All the wranglers were there, surrounding the corral, most likely for moral support, she thought. Taking a place between Wade and Billy, Ena watched Mitch hanging on to a dapple-gray stallion. There was a great deal of daylight between Mitch and the saddle as the stallion bucked like crazy, trying to get Mitch off his back.

"Why is Mitch on top of that horse?" she cried, directing her question toward Wade. Ena couldn't look away, afraid that at any second, Mitch was going to go flying into the air. She could feel her heart climbing up higher into her throat, lodging itself there.

"Best way anyone knows to break in a horse," Wade replied calmly.

"Shouldn't someone else be doing this instead of Mitch?" Ena asked. If anything happened to him, the Double E would be out a foreman—among other things. This was just crazy, she thought.

"Nobody's better when it comes to breaking horses than Mitch," Billy piped up. It was evident that the younger hand had a serious case of hero worship when it came to the foreman.

"Don't worry," Wade assured her, sensing her agitation. "Mitch knows what he's doing."

She was clutching the top rail of the fence and her knuckles were turning white. She wasn't even aware of breathing.

Ena never took her eyes off the bucking horse and his rider.

"What he's doing is rattling around what few brains he's got in that head of his," Ena declared angrily, her voice rising as the stallion became more and more frenzied.

"This isn't Mitch's first rodeo—or his first bucking bronco," Wade told her, adding confidently, "He's gonna be fine." Then, as some of the others gasped, Wade cried, "Wow!" when Mitch looked as if he was about to rise up even higher from his mount and was in danger of literally going flying. "That was a close one!"

With each attempt, the horse, aptly named Wildfire, seemed more determined than ever to throw off the man on his back. Bucking and tossing his head, Wildfire's frenzy grew in scope.

And then, with one more incredible upward leap, Wildfire threw Mitch off.

Ena screamed as Mitch hit the ground, watching in horror as the back of his head bounced as it made contact with the hard dirt.

For a dreadful second, the foreman appeared to be too stunned to get up.

Nobody moved.

Not waiting for any of the ranch hands gathered around the perimeter to do anything, Ena maneuvered herself through the space in the corral's railings. But before she could run to Mitch, Wade had caught her by the arm.

Frustrated, she tried to yank her arm away and looked at the older man accusingly.

"Give him a minute," Wade counseled.

"To do what? Get stomped on?" Ena cried angrily. "He's lying there like some kind of rag doll. He's a *target*," she pointed out, exasperated.

Turning back, she saw Mitch shake his head as if to clear it. Then, moving quickly, he caught hold of the stallion's dragging reins and pulled Wildfire back. That threw the animal off balance for a split second. Mitch used that sliver of time to climb back into the stallion's saddle.

Ena watched, horrified. "Is he crazy?" she demanded, looking from Wade to Billy.

"If he doesn't get back up on the horse, that stallion is going to be twice as hard to break," Wade told her matter-of-factly, never taking his eyes off the resilient foreman.

"So one horse doesn't get broken. At least Mitch

won't break his neck—or worse," Ena said, not understanding what the big deal was.

"Mr. Mitch isn't going to accept that," Billy told her solemnly. "Mr. Mitch never met a horse he couldn't break," the young wrangler added proudly.

"Make sure you write that on his tombstone," Ena said, disgusted.

But angry as she was at what she viewed to be a stupid move on Mitch's part, she couldn't get herself to tear her eyes away from the horse and his would-be master. She caught herself praying that Mitch wouldn't come flying off the horse again. This time he was liable to split his head wide open.

The minutes ticked by. Wildfire bucked less and less until, eventually, the horse grew tired of trying to throw Mitch off his back altogether and surrendered. The last couple of minutes, the once-wild horse became totally docile. Triumphant, Mitch allowed Wildfire one final peaceful go-round as the horse moved along the perimeter of the corral.

Billy ran up to Mitch and eagerly took the reins from the foreman's hand as the latter slid off the newly tamed stallion's back.

"I *knew* you could do it, sir," Billy told him, beaming.

Ena was right on the hired hand's heels, less than a half beat behind him. She did a quick survey of the man standing in front of her. Something was off—she could feel it.

"Are you all right?" she demanded, still looking at Mitch.

"Never better," he responded, flashing a satisfied grin. "Why?"

"Because I watched you smash your head," she told him impatiently.

"Oh, that's nothing," he said, waving away her concern. "It's a hard head," he laughed.

One of the men called to him and Mitch turned to look in his direction. He turned a little too quickly and seemed to waver a little unsteadily on his feet.

Ena saw his face turn slightly pale. He stood very still for a second, as if he was trying to regain his balance.

"Are you all right?" Ena repeated, growing really concerned.

"I said I'm fine," Mitch insisted.

"And I just saw you turn pale right in front of me," Ena countered.

He could see the men looking at him, probably not knowing what to think. He had to put this to rest. "Must be your imagination," he replied, shrugging off her concern.

But Ena wasn't about to be put off. Drawing closer to him, her eyes narrowed as she looked into his. "I don't think so. You came down really hard when you hit your head."

"It's not the first time," he told her glibly. "All part of the work."

"You could be walking around with a concussion," she said pointedly, getting in front of him so he couldn't walk away from her.

His smile was tolerant. "Why don't you let me worry about that?" he said. Then, looking over her head toward Wade, he said, "Wade, where's the other horse you wanted me to break?"

Wade began to answer, then saw the warning look in Ena's eyes. He quickly improvised. "The horse was taken back to his stall."

"This is the first I've heard of it. Why?" Mitch asked.

"Um, he didn't look all that well to me," Wade told him, saying the first thing that came to his mind. He shrugged helplessly. "Why don't you take a break from taming the horses for today?"

For the first time, Ena saw Mitch getting annoyed. "What, she get to you, too?"

"She's making sense, sir," Billy said, timidly adding his voice to Wade's. "You did hit the ground pretty hard, sir."

"Right. I'm the one who fell so I should know how hard I hit the ground and I said I was fine, damn it!" Mitch insisted.

But the next move Mitch made completely contradicted his assertion. Turning away from Wade, Billy and the woman who he felt had put them up to this, Mitch felt his knees almost buckle right under him.

Grasping the first thing he could reach so that he could remain upright, he wound up clutching Ena's shoulder.

That made her point, Ena thought.

"I think we both know that I'm right." She glanced at Wade and Billy. "Can I get you two to watch him while I go get the truck?" she asked.

Second-guessing her intent, Billy said, "We can get him back to the house for you, ma'am."

"Thank you but I'm not going back to the house," Ena told the younger wrangler. "I'm taking Mitch into town so he can see one of the doctors at the clinic."

Mitch stiffened. "I don't need to see a doctor," he protested.

"Maybe not," Ena replied and for a second Mitch looked relieved. But not for long. "But the doctor needs to see you. It's called taking precautions."

"It's called a waste of time," he countered, frustrated.

"Po-ta-toe, po-tah-toe," Ena responded. Then she added, "Humor me."

"Look, thanks for your concern, really, but I don't have time for this," Mitch told her.

He shut his eyes for a second because things were spinning. Mercifully, when he opened his eyes, the world had settled down again.

But Ena looked as determined as ever to get him to the doctor.

Completely unaffected by Mitch's protests, Ena calmly said, "We're making time for this." She looked at the two men she was entrusting to remain with Mitch. "Watch him," she ordered. "Tie him up if you have to. I'll be right back."

"You know that this is totally unnecessary!" Mitch said, calling after her. "I'm really fine!" He craned his neck so that his voice would carry as she hurried away from the corral.

Ena was back faster than he had anticipated. She was driving his truck.

"What did you do, run?" he asked.

"As a matter of fact, I did," she said, sounding a little breathless as she got out of the cab of the truck. "I was afraid you'd bully these guys into letting you just walk away. And before you say anything about the cost, don't worry. I'm going to take care of it."

"It's totally unnecessary," Mitch maintained. "If you have your heart set on throwing your money away, you can do it by paying off some of those accounts for the Double E that you said were in arrears."

"I am working on that," she assured him. "But just as important as paying off the accounts is having a living, breathing foreman. Get him into the truck, boys," she said, addressing Wade and Billy.

"I can get in on my own," Mitch retorted, pulling back from the two wranglers.

Ena shot him a look that said she was coming to the end of her patience. "Then do it!"

"Lady sounds like she means business to me," Wade told Mitch. "Don't worry, I'll hold down the fort while you're gone."

He was talking to Mitch, but it was Ena who responded, "I appreciate that."

"Well, I don't," Mitch said, speaking up as Wade hustled him into the passenger side of the truck.

"You don't count right now," she told him just as she climbed up into the driver's seat. Seated, she looked out the window at Wade and Billy, as well as the others. "I'll be back as soon as I can," she promised.

"Hey, this is my truck, you know," Mitch pointed out indignantly.

"I know," she replied, putting the key into the ignition again.

"Well, if you know that, then why are you driving it?" he asked.

She didn't want to say anything in front of his men because he might feel that she was undermining him. But now that they were alone, she could tell him the reason she was so concerned. "Because one of your pupils is dilated and a lot bigger than the other one."

He had no idea what that meant or why she thought it was a reason to be dragging him off to the medical clinic. "What? What does that even mean?"

"It means that you might have a concussion and I want to get you checked out to make sure that we're not ignoring something serious."

He sighed. "Concussion again," he repeated in disgust.

"Yup. And I'll keep saying that word until the doctor can rule it out," Ena told him.

"I don't remember you being this stubborn when we were in high school together," he told her.

"Well, guess what? I am," she said brightly.

He crossed his arms in front of his chest, the picture of the immovable object—or so he hoped. "We're going to be stuck at that medical clinic all day and maybe I won't get in to see the doctor anyway."

"That's okay. We'll take our chances," she said philosophically. She'd started driving toward Forever, but the truck bucked a little before it got back into gear. "What's wrong with this thing?"

"It doesn't like strangers driving it," he answered without any hesitation.

"Too bad," she told him. Glancing over toward him, Ena saw that Mitch hadn't put his seat belt on. "Buckle up, cowboy."

"Why? Am I in for a bumpy ride?" he asked dryly, quoting an obscure movie reference he remembered having heard once.

The smile she threw him sent a chill down along his spine. "You have no idea," she promised, pressing down on the accelerator.

The medical clinic was crowded, just as he had predicted. Debi, one of the two nurses who were coordinating the various patients seated in the waiting area, looked up from her computer and asked, "May I help you?"

Ena had no qualms about telling the young woman, "Yes, this is an emergency."

"Are you hurt?" Debi asked, quickly scrutinizing her.

"I'm not, but—" Ena lowered her voice because she knew that Mitch wouldn't want anyone overhearing the reason she had dragged him in to see the doctor "—he was breaking in a horse and the horse threw him. He flew off and hit his head. One of his pupils is dilated."

Mitch closed in on Ena. "She's worrying needlessly," he told Debi.

"Why don't we let one of the doctors determine that?" Debi suggested kindly. "I think that Dr. Dan is up next, unless you'd rather see—"

"Dr. Dan will be fine," Mitch said, eager to get out of there. "But really, this isn't necessary. I've got work to do."

"And we're going to get you doing it as soon as possible." Debi looked around at the waiting room and rose slightly in her chair to get a better look. "You folks mind if I squeeze Mitch here in ahead of you?" she asked the patients waiting to be seen.

Ena braced herself to try to appeal to these people, some of whom she recognized but others were complete strangers to her.

She had prepared herself needlessly, however, because the people in the waiting room quickly gave their permission, willingly stepping back so that the cowboy they all knew could go in first.

"Sure, he can have my spot," one man toward the back of the reception room said.

"I certainly don't mind waiting," a young woman told Debi.

"Got nothing waiting for me at home except for Carrie, who is dying to tell me I told you so, so sure, he can go in ahead of me," an older man responded, waving Mitch in.

"I knew your dad." Another man spoke up, looking at Ena. "He would have wanted me to let Mitch here go in if he's hurt."

"I'm not hurt," Mitch insisted, raising his voice to get his point across.

"That's what we're trying to determine," Ena reminded him. "If you don't have a concussion, you can give me all the grief about it you want on the way back. If you do have one, then I get to say I told you so and your soul is mine," she told him.

"Hey, that sure sounds like a fair bargain to me," an older woman said, then cackled at the possible outcome of the confrontation.

"Looks like you get to go in next, Mitch," Debi told him, coming around toward him from behind her desk. "Just follow me."

"I'll wait here," Ena told him.

She would have preferred going into the exam room with him, but she knew she couldn't very well go in and hold his hand. He wouldn't stand for it, and besides, she wasn't related to him.

She watched Debi lead Mitch in through the door that led to the exam rooms in the back of the clinic.

With a sigh, she moved away from the reception desk and found a seat in the waiting room.

Chapter Fourteen

"Waiting is always the hardest part, honey."

The remark came from an older woman sitting in the waiting room. The woman was to Ena's right and she leaned forward in her seat to give their exchange a semblance of privacy. Smiling, the woman patted Ena's hand as if they had some sort of bond between them, even though Ena didn't recognize her.

Ena forced a smile to her lips. "I guess it is," she replied politely.

"Oh, I know it is because you're stuck out here, letting your imagination run wild. If you were in there with him, asking questions and finding things out, it would be a lot easier for you, trust me," the woman told her with confidence. Her face brightened. "But he'll be out by and by."

Ena forced a smile to her lips and just nodded in response.

The smile the woman flashed at Ena was genuine. "You don't remember me, do you?"

Ena had to admit that the woman's voice sounded vaguely familiar, but her face wasn't. Ena shook her head. "I'm sorry—"

The matronly-looking woman laughed. "Oh, don't be sorry, dear. The last time I saw you, I had brown hair instead of all this gray and you were this cute little senior going to high school along with my daughter, Sandra."

The name instantly triggered a memory. "Mrs. Baker?" Ena cried uncertainly, looking more closely at the woman in the waiting room.

Shirley Baker laughed, delighted. "So, you do remember me."

"Of course I do," Ena answered, genuine pleasure filling her voice. "How's Sandra doing?" she asked, grateful to be able to actually carry on a conversation instead of doing what the woman had said, letting her mind come up with awful scenarios about Mitch's possible condition.

Mrs. Baker beamed. "Sandra's doing just great. She's married now. Gave me two beautiful grandbabies," the woman said proudly. "They're two and four. I watch them for her when she works at the hotel. I'm taking the day off today, getting my semiannual with the doctor," she confided in a lower voice. And then she went on to say in a louder voice, "We've done a lot of growing here in Forever since you've been gone."

Ena nodded. "I noticed."

Shirley Baker's expression turned sympathetic. "I was sorry to hear about your dad. He was a good man. A lot of people came to his funeral," she said, obviously thinking Ena would take comfort in that. "Almost everyone in town paid their respects."

"So everyone keeps telling me." Because this woman was someone she had once known, Ena knew the woman was undoubtedly wondering why she hadn't attended her father's funeral. "I didn't know he was ill until he was gone," she started to explain.

Mrs. Baker reached over and squeezed Ena's hand. "Nobody's blaming you, dear. Family ties aren't always the easiest to maintain," she told Ena. "I just wanted you to know that when my Henry died, your dad was the first one at my door, managing things for me until I could get my head together and deal with things myself. I don't know where I would have been without him."

"My father did that?" Ena asked incredulously.

She couldn't remember a single instance over the years when her father actually went out with friends or, for that matter, even mentioned having any. How had that solitary man transformed himself into the perennial good neighbor?

Mrs. Baker nodded. "Your father."

"When I fell off my tractor and wound up breaking my leg, it was your dad who came over every day after he finished his own work to help out with mine. And when he couldn't come over, he sent that foreman of his over. The one you brought in to see the doc," Jeb Russell told her, adding his voice to Shirley Baker's.

That started the ball rolling. Within minutes, other people in the waiting room were speaking up, telling Ena about things that her father had selflessly done for them when they found themselves suddenly in need of a good neighbor.

Ena felt both stunned and overwhelmed. It was hard for her to reconcile this version of her father with the one she had grown up with and had always known. She felt cheated because he had never been this way with her and he had never allowed her to witness what was obviously a new, improved version of Bruce O'Rourke.

After she had left home, the man *had* reinvented himself.

Why this new, improved version never attempted to get in touch with her—especially after he had had her tracked down—was still very much a mystery to her. Yes, Mitch had given her a reason, but it was a relatively poor one and it didn't really begin to provide her with any answers to her questions.

When the door leading to the examination rooms in the rear of the medical clinic opened and Mitch came out, Ena was busy talking to another one of the patients. She didn't see him at first. When she did, she immediately shot up to her feet and quickly crossed over to the reception desk.

She saw a tall kind-looking man in a white lab coat talking to Mitch. He had to be the doctor, she decided. Why was he still talking to Mitch?

Was something else wrong?

Apprehension immediately returned to her in spades as she came closer.

"How is he?" she asked the man in the lab coat without any preamble.

Dr. Daniel Davenport turned his head in her direction. "You must be Ena O'Rourke," he said, putting out his hand to her.

Ena shook his hand without really taking note of what she was doing. She was completely focused on Mitch. "I am. How is he?" she repeated.

"You're right," Dan said to Mitch, who was standing right next to him. "She is really is as direct as her father was."

Ena immediately wanted to deny the similarity, but doing so would take her down another path and she didn't want to distract the doctor. She wanted her question answered.

Now.

Rephrasing her question, she asked, "Does he have a concussion?"

"I did a CAT scan. He does have a concussion, but it is only a very mild one," Dan told her.

Mitch appeared vindicated. "See, I told you I didn't have to come in," he said to her.

Dan continued talking as if Mitch hadn't said a word. "But you were right to bring him in," he said to Ena. "It's better to check these things out than to experience regrets later on." He glanced toward Mitch, then told Ena, "I'd definitely recommend a couple of days of rest for him."

"Rest. Got it," Ena said as if she was making the doctor a promise. "Anything else?" She wasn't about to rely on Mitch to tell her the doctor's instructions once they left here.

"He should be all right after that," Dan responded. "But if he experiences any complications—dizziness, nausea, trouble sleeping, that sort of thing," he elaborated, "I want you to call the clinic immediately and bring him back here."

"We won't have to make that call," Mitch told the doctor.

"Unless we do," Ena said, overruling Mitch.

Dan laughed quietly as he watched the couple leave his waiting room.

"I'd say that he's met his match. What do you think?" he asked the nurse.

"I think that you're right, Doctor," Debi told him, then handed Dan the medical file for the next patient waiting to see him.

"See, I told you that there was nothing to worry about," Mitch said as they walked back to his truck in the parking lot.

"That is *not* what I heard the doctor say," Ena responded.

"Maybe you should have had your ears checked while we were there," Mitch suggested.

Reaching his truck, he was about to open the driver's-side door. Ena managed to block his hand with her own, keeping him from opening the door.

"What are you doing?" Mitch asked, looking at her in confusion.

"I'll drive," she informed him.

Mitch was far from pleased. "The doc said I was okay."

"No, he said you had a mild concussion and to watch you for a couple of days," Ena corrected. "The man said nothing about watching you drive," she stressed. "Now, get into the truck on the passenger side—unless you want to stand here for the better part of the day and argue about it."

Mitch sighed and shook his head, then stopped abruptly, the color suddenly completely draining from his face.

Ena was instantly alert. "Did you just get dizzy?"

He expected her to gloat or utter those awful words: *I told you so.* When she didn't and exhibited concern instead, Mitch decided that maybe he should stop giving her a hard time. He acted grateful instead.

"Maybe I will sit in the passenger seat for now," he told her.

"Good choice," she agreed. She waited for Mitch to climb into the truck on the other side, fighting the urge to offer her help. She already felt she knew how he would react to that. "Ready?" she asked once he'd closed his door and buckled up.

"For your driving?" he quipped, covering up the fact that, just for a second, he'd felt dizzy again. "Not really."

Ena got in on the driver's side. "I'll have you know that I'm a very good driver."

"You forget, I've already had a sample of your driving. I was with you when you drove to the clinic," he reminded her. "Dallas must have different driving standards than we do."

"Dallas," she informed him coolly, "has decent roads."

"Does that mean that you don't speed there?" he asked, feigning surprise.

"I *didn't* speed to the clinic," she told him. "I was just trying to get you to the doctor before you could come up with a reason to bail on me," she informed him stiffly.

"Does that mean that you're going to be taking your time driving back to the ranch?" he questioned.

"Now that we know all you really need is some bed rest," she said, easing back on the accelerator, "yes, I'm going to be taking my time getting back to the Double E."

Mitch frowned when she mentioned bed rest.

"If you're expecting me to just lie around for the next two days—" he began.

Ena cut him off. "Yes, that's *exactly* what I'm expecting."

"Then I suggest you prepare yourself to be disappointed. I've got far too much to do to lie around like a lump for two days."

Her eyes narrowed. "I can have you tied to your bed."

For a second, he allowed himself to build on that image, but then, shaking it off, he said, "As tempting as that sounds, no, I'll have to pass on that."

"Did I give you the impression that this was up for a vote?" she asked. "If I did, then I'm sorry because it's not. You have no say in this. It's just me and the doctor." And then she relented. "We can compromise, and you can be on my dad's old recliner instead of a bed."

She had noticed the old chair the other day. It was shoved over in a corner of the living room. She could clean it up so that Mitch could use it.

"It's only a compromise if you put that recliner out in the middle of the corral so I can do the work I signed on for," he informed her.

"If you're going to give me a hard time," she fired back in a steely tone, "I wasn't kidding about having you tied up."

He laughed shortly at her threat. "Sorry, I don't mean to insult you but you're not strong enough to do that."

She was not the weakling he took her to be, Ena thought. "You'd be surprised," she told him. Then she went on to say, "But who says I was going to be the one to tie you up?" When she saw the perplexed expression on his face, she told him, "I'll get Wade, Billy and Felicity to hold you down and tie you up—and if they're not enough, I can always call in Miss Joan. If anyone can *make* you rest, it's Miss Joan."

He sighed. "Okay, Uncle," he cried, surrendering. "You win."

Ena laughed. "I figured threatening you with Miss Joan would tip the scales in my favor. This is for your own good," she told Mitch.

He was cornered and he knew it. There was no use in fighting the matter. Even so, Mitch blew out a frustrated breath.

"You really are a lot like your father," he told Ena. He saw her stiffen. "That's not a bad thing, you know."

"So I've been hearing," she said with a touch of exasperation in her voice. She still hadn't made her peace with the fact that her father had made this transformation *after* she had left town. "Those people in the waiting room, they all told me about what a good man my father was, how helpful he was, volunteering to help his neighbors when they needed him."

"He was and he did," Mitch affirmed.

"Where was this version of him when I was growing up?" she asked.

"I really can't answer that for you," Mitch admitted. "He was being busy, I guess. Maybe being overwhelmed by all the things he was trying to do. What matters, in the end, was the man that he became." He hoped she could take some comfort in that.

But it was obvious that she didn't. "I wouldn't know about that."

"I can tell you about him," Mitch volunteered. "So can some of the others on the ranch."

"When we get to the ranch, you're going to be resting, remember?" Ena reminded him.

"The doctor didn't say anything about resting my jaw muscle," he said.

"I'll place a call to the doctor when we get home,"

she said with such a straight face, he didn't know if she was being serious. "Maybe he just forgot to mention that little thing."

There was silence for a few minutes as Ena continued to drive, and then Mitch spoke. "I'm probably going to regret this…" he began, then stopped for a beat.

"Regret what?" she asked when he didn't continue.

"Saying this," he told her.

"Saying what?" she asked impatiently. The man could draw out a single syllable.

He took a deep breath, as if he needed the extra air to push the word out of his mouth. And then he finally told her, "Thanks."

"You're thanking me? For dragging your stubborn hide into town and to the doctor?" she guessed.

"No," he admitted, "for caring enough to see that something was off."

"Then you *are* dizzy," she said triumphantly because he'd finally admitted it.

"Was," Mitch corrected. "And I'll admit that it might not have been the worst idea to have me checked out. The doc told me that he'd seen a few of these cases go sideways."

Ena smiled. "So, let me get this straight. You agree that I did a good thing, overruling you and bringing you in to get checked out, is that it?" she asked him. He could hear the smile in her voice.

"Don't let it go to your head," he warned.

Her smile widened, her eyes crinkling as she spared him a look. "Too late."

Mitch sighed, feigning aggravation. "I knew I was going to regret this."

"Not as much as if we hadn't gone in and you suddenly started experiencing all the complications that go along with a head injury," she said seriously.

"This seems to be a personal crusade of yours," he commented.

"In a way, I guess it is." She paused for a moment, debating whether or not to share something with Mitch. To be honest, she was surprised he didn't already know, seeing how close he'd gotten to her father. "My uncle— my dad's younger brother—got thrown from a horse when I was a kid. He wasn't even trying to tame it. The horse was spooked by a rattler, reared, and my uncle just fell off. Hit his head, thought nothing of it and shook it off. A week later, he was dead," she said flatly, holding thoughts of the incident at bay. After all these years, the memory still hurt just as sharply as it had that day. "The doc at the hospital said the injury had caused a blood vessel to break and he bled out." She paused for a long moment before she could continue. Glancing at Mitch, she told him, "I just wanted to be sure that didn't happen to you."

"Oh. Well, thanks for that," he mumbled.

"Yeah, just remember that when I tell you to rest," she said.

This time he kept the words that rose to his lips in response to himself. He figured he owed it to her.

Chapter Fifteen

"This isn't necessary, you know," Mitch insisted as he watched Ena making up the sofa in the spare bedroom.

She didn't even bother stopping what she was doing to look in his direction. Instead, she focused on turning the sagging sofa into something that she would be able to sleep on.

His late boss's daughter had to be the most stubborn woman he had ever encountered, Mitch thought. He tried dissuading her one more time, although he had a feeling it was futile.

"I'm perfectly capable of spending the night in my bunk at the bunkhouse," he told her. "Or, if you don't trust me, I can sack out on the recliner."

When they had returned from the medical clinic, Ena had covered the faded leather chair with a sheet, as well as a comforter. Mitch had grudgingly spent the rest of the day there.

However, he had to admit that he had enjoyed having Ena make him dinner. She'd insisted that he eat that in the recliner, as well. Because Felicity had the afternoon off, Ena had made the meal—boiled chicken along with a bowl of homemade chicken soup. Mitch felt as if he were five years old again, but it was nice to be fussed over, although he would have never admitted it out loud.

But now, in his opinion, she was really going too far.

"You're sleeping here," she told him with finality as she finished making up the sofa. "And so am I."

Mitch blinked, wondering if he was hallucinating or if his hearing was suddenly going. He swallowed because his mouth had gone dry. "How's that again?"

"You heard me," she told him, turning around to look at him. "I'm sleeping in here."

That caught him completely off guard. He thought of the times he'd fantasized about just this sort of thing when they were back in high school. "Not that I mind," he told her in a hoarse voice. "But why?"

"I want to be here in case you have a seizure during the night," she said matter-of-factly.

"A what?" He stared at her. Was she kidding? But one look at her face and he saw she was serious. "Look, I appreciate you being concerned, but you've been watching way too many doctor programs on TV," he insisted. "I told you, I'm fine."

"Yes, I know what you keep saying," she replied. "But the doctor said you have a mild concussion." She waved at the sofa. "This is just precautionary. But if, during the night, you suddenly have a seizure or start throwing up, someone has to be here to look after you. Although it pains me to say it, none of those guys in the bunkhouse would know the first thing to do if that does happen."

He looked at her rather skeptically. "Oh, and you do?"

"Yes, I do," she informed him, adding, "I've had some first aid training."

Mitch wasn't sure if he believed her, but he supposed it was possible. He let her words sink in.

"Wow, you're just full of surprises, aren't you?" he marveled, giving her the benefit of the doubt.

She knew what he was trying to do—and she wasn't about to be diverted. "Don't turn this around, Parnell. We're talking about you, not me."

She was like a bulldog, he thought. Once she latched onto something, he couldn't shake her loose.

He decided to try another approach. "So I'm getting the bed and you're getting that lumpy thing over there that's supposed to pass as a sofa, is that it?" He frowned, looking at it. "That doesn't look very comfortable."

"Don't worry about me," she said, dismissing his observation.

Mitch looked thoughtfully at the double bed that was up against one wall. "You know, this bed's big enough to accommodate two people."

"Whatever you're thinking, Parnell, it's not happening," she informed him. "The whole idea of all this is for you to get some rest, not get yourself all worked up."

And that was as close to the subject of lovemaking as she intended to get—at least until he was completely out of the woods.

"We could each stay on our side of the bed," Mitch proposed, not ready to abandon the subject just yet.

She refused to allow herself to be tempted—even though she was. "This isn't a negotiation."

"So you're just going to be a dictator now?" Mitch asked.

It would have been more effective without the mischievous smile, she thought. Doing her best to sound tough, she said, "Watch me."

That was just the problem. He had been watching her. A lot. And the more he watched her, the more he found himself wanting her. Having her hovering over him like this, ministering to him, only made his longing grow that much stronger.

"You know," he said, lowering his voice seductively, "I usually sleep in the nude."

Now he was just saying anything to get a rise out of her, Ena thought. She would have known about a pajamaless sleeping habit if Mitch actually had one. There were no such things as secrets on the ranch. But for the moment, she pretended to believe him. "Not tonight you're not."

Resigned, Mitch gave up and lay back in the bed.

"All right," he told her. "You win."

"The outcome was never in doubt," she informed him. "See you in the morning, Mitch," she said, lying down on the sofa and shutting off the lamp on the side table. The room was suddenly bathed in darkness.

"You're sleeping in your clothes?" Mitch questioned. He was still dressed himself, but that was only because he'd been hoping to retreat back to the bunkhouse before she had become a human watchdog.

"I am tonight," she answered.

Ena tried to fluff up her pillow. It wasn't cooperating. Neither was the sagging sofa. It wasn't easy finding a comfortable position on it.

Mitch could hear her moving around and guessed

that the sofa was even more uncomfortable than she had bargained on.

"Offer still stands," he told her. "There's plenty of room in the bed."

"Go to sleep, Parnell," Ena ordered.

"Yes, ma'am."

"And stop grinning," she said. "I can hear the grin in your voice."

Which only made him smile more. But he dutifully said, "Yes, ma'am."

Ena remained awake for a while, anticipating any one of a number of things. But eventually, the sound of Mitch's even breathing lulled her to sleep.

The night went by without any further incident.

Ena had had every intention to get up before Mitch was awake. But when she finally opened her eyes, the first thing she was aware of was that Mitch had his head propped up on his fisted hand and he was looking at her.

Intently.

She frowned as she instantly sat up, still not totally conscious. She dragged her fingers through her hair, doing what she could to make herself appear presentable. It was hopeless, she decided.

She fixed Mitch with a glare. "Why aren't you still sleeping?"

"Because I'm an early riser," he replied. He'd been awake for a while and had spent the time just watching her sleep. "Do you know that you wrinkle your nose when you're sleeping?"

"I'll be sure to make a note of that," she replied crisply.

But Mitch wasn't finished with his observation yet. "It's kind of cute."

She supposed he was just trying to be nice. "Glad you approve of my wrinkled nose. More important, how are you feeling?"

He looked at her. "Like a slug who wants to get back to work."

Ena nodded, taking his answer in stride. "In other words, normal."

"Yes," he said, seizing on the word. "Normal!" All he wanted was for her to treat him as if everything was back to normal.

"Good." She smiled sweetly at him as she kicked off the covers and got off the sofa. "Then you have one more day to go."

Mitch gave her an exasperated look. "Ena O'Rourke, you are a cruel woman."

She wasn't doing this to win points with him. "Cruel or not, the doctor said to have you rest for a couple of days and we're sticking to that."

"I warn you, I'm going to go stir-crazy," he complained as he watched her head toward the room's doorway.

"Nobody ever went stir-crazy in two days," she assured him.

His mood grew just the slightest bit more desperate. "Then I'll be the first."

"You know, you could try being patient," she told Mitch.

He'd already thrown off his own covers and was sitting on the edge of the bed, itching to get moving. "Not in my nature."

"Learn," she told him as she left the room. "I'm going to see about breakfast."

Refusing to remain confined, Mitch brushed his

teeth, threw some water on his face and went down into the kitchen.

She'd expected him to protest, then give in the way he had yesterday. But that didn't seem to be happening, she thought when she saw him coming into the kitchen.

"What are you doing here?" Ena asked.

"Stretching my legs," he lied. "I was getting cramps in them because of all that *resting* I was doing."

Felicity, busy making breakfast, looked thoughtfully from Ena to the foreman who had just walked into her domain. She didn't ask any questions, but it was obvious from the look on her face that she was filling in the blanks for herself.

"Hungry?" she asked Mitch.

Mitch grinned. That was a question that he could answer without hesitation. "Starving."

The housekeeper nodded. "That is a good sign," she said with approval.

Ena had told the housekeeper about Mitch's visit to the medical center the moment she saw the woman. She was attempting to enlist Felicity's help.

"The doctor said he should rest," she insisted.

Felicity glanced over at the foreman. "And by the looks of him, he did. But too much rest makes a person feel useless and lazy. That is no way to run a ranch," the housekeeper concluded with authority.

Ena threw up her hands, knowing she couldn't fight both Felicity and Mitch.

"All right, if you promise not to exert yourself and to let the other hands do all the heavy stuff, you don't have to go back to bed after you eat. Good enough?" she asked Mitch.

The smile he flashed her caused her stomach to

tighten as a little thrill worked its way down her spine. It almost made her surrender worth it.

If she worried that the others would rag on Mitch for allowing himself to be restricted by her, she could have saved herself the grief. When the ranch hands saw him that morning, they greeted Mitch as if he were a conquering hero coming home from war.

Things quickly went back to normal after that. Mitch couldn't have been happier.

Because she had allowed her other responsibilities—both the accounts from her firm as well as the accounts in her father's poor excuse for a ledger—slide, she began putting in more time working on them. So much so that she was back to losing sleep because she stayed up late and was up early, doing her best to attempt to catch up.

At times it began to feel like a losing battle, but she wasn't about to give up, even though she felt herself fading.

Every shred of time she had was utilized.

"Hey, ever hear that old chestnut 'Physician, heal thyself'?" Mitch asked her one evening several weeks later.

He was standing in the doorway of the study, watching her working after she had already put in a full day's work on the ranch. Something stirred within him. Damn, but he had never gotten over her, he thought.

He walked into the room.

"I'm aware of it," she told Mitch without looking up. Having put in time on her firm's accounts, she was back to trying to figure out what to do about rectifying her father's rather creative record keeping.

"Then maybe you should think about giving it a try," he said.

"Later," she responded. "If you hadn't noticed, I'm busy right now."

"I noticed," he answered. "Seems to me that you're busy all the time."

She was getting cross-eyed, trying to follow the numbers on the page. "Uh-huh."

"You're not listening to me, are you?" he asked.

"Uh-huh."

That was what he thought. This time, he put his hand down on the ledger, blocking her view.

"Hey!" she cried in protest, looking at him.

He could be just as stubborn as she was, Mitch thought. And this was for her own good. "You need a break."

"What I *need* is to get this done," she countered, physically removing his hand from the ledger.

He could have kept his hand there if he wanted to. Instead, he let her move it. But he needed to get her to see things his way—for her own good.

"You're going to make yourself sick, you know that. You're not just burning the candle at both ends—you're burning the candle in the middle, too," Mitch insisted.

She closed her eyes, searching for strength. "Thank you for your concern, but—"

Mitch didn't let her finish. "Does this conversation sound familiar to you?" he asked. Because she didn't say anything, he went on, "Let me refresh your memory for you—you and I had this exact same conversation a few weeks ago, except I was the one being lectured and I was the one insisting I was fine. You, in your infinite wisdom, pointed out that I wasn't." He looked directly into her eyes. "Allow me to return the favor now," he requested.

Ena sighed, knowing Mitch was right. That didn't

make it any easier for her to back off. "You can be a royal pain, you know."

He grinned at her and said, "Right back at you."

Dead tired, she still made an attempt to reason with him. "Look, I can let the accounts from my old firm go for the time being. I can say that I've decided to take a prolonged vacation and focus on the ranch for now—but that hodgepodge that my father called a ledger? I can't just ignore that. Too many things are coming due soon and if I don't find a way to get creative and to manage to secure an extension on the bank's note, the ranch is going to be under new ownership and it's not going to be mine, Parnell."

He looked at her thoughtfully. "Maybe you can find a way to make the bank give you that extension you mentioned. The bank really doesn't want your ranch. It's more profitable for them if you keep the ranch and repay the loan."

Ena scrubbed her hands over her face and then looked at Mitch. "You know, for a cowboy, you think like an accountant."

"I'll pretend you didn't say that," Mitch told her, keeping a straight face. "Look, there's a party this weekend. I know for a fact that the bank manager is going to be there. Maybe if we approach him in a friendly, neutral setting, he might be open to seeing things your way. Maybe you'll even come up with a viable suggestion about a repayment schedule by then."

She hadn't gotten past the first sentence. "A party?"

He nodded. "Miss Joan's holding the party for Dr. Dan and his wife. It's celebrating the clinic being open for ten years. Everyone's invited," he added before she could protest that she hadn't gotten an invitation so she couldn't go. "You wouldn't want to insult Miss Joan by not attending."

She rolled her eyes. "Heaven forbid."

"Not to mention the fact that you could use the break," he told her. "By my count, you've been doing nothing but work ever since you got here and you above all people know that you need to balance that out," he told her.

"I balance it out," she protested. When he looked at her, she told him, "I sleep."

"Not much fun in that," Mitch told her. "C'mon, you'll be killing two birds with one stone. You'll be approaching the bank manager on neutral ground and you'll be getting some much-needed recreation. You know what they say, all work and no play, et cetera."

Ena raised her eyes to his. "Are you saying that I'm dull?" she asked, playing out the rest of the saying in her head.

Mitch smiled at her, his eyes saying things to her that he couldn't say out loud.

Her breath caught in her throat as she tried to ignore the way her pulse had picked up, responding to the way he was looking at her—and making her want things that would only cause problems in the long run.

"No, I'd never say you were dull," he told her. "Anything but dull," he added with enthusiasm, his words all but caressing her face.

"Is that a compliment, Parnell, or am I just being extremely punchy?" she asked.

"That was a compliment," he assured her. "You are the most well-rounded, fascinating woman I have ever met and I certainly wouldn't think of insulting you," Mitch said. He cleared his throat before he said anything else. "So, about that party…" He allowed his voice to trail off as he waited for her to agree.

She sighed. "When did you say it was?"

Mitch knew that meant yes. "This Saturday."

Ena shrugged. "All right, I'll go. For the good of the ranch—and not to insult Miss Joan."

His grin widened. "Good idea."

Chapter Sixteen

Mitch glanced up at the sky. He was able to tell time by the position of the sun as easily as if he were looking at his watch. Right now, it was getting late.

"We'd better start getting ready if we're going to make that party that Miss Joan's throwing," he said to Ena as he stripped off his gloves. He shoved them into his back pocket and started to head out of the corral.

"Yeah, about that," Ena replied slowly, deliberately avoiding Mitch's eyes. She always felt as if his piercing blue eyes could see right through her and she really didn't want to deal with that right now.

Looking at the ground, she told him, "I'm not going." When Mitch said nothing in response, she could feel herself beginning to fidget inside. She was anticipating an argument. "A party's no place to talk business, and besides, there's just too much to do here." She waved her hand at the straw they had been spreading around in the stalls that was a long way from finished. "I can't just take off and play hooky for the better part of the day. What if something goes wrong?"

More silence.

She pressed her lips together, already knowing what he had to say about that. "Okay, so the hands might be able to handle it, but I'd still rather be here myself—just in case," she insisted.

Running out of words, Ena finally looked up at Mitch. The man could be so infuriating.

"Well? Aren't you going to say *anything*?" she asked.

The foreman looked at her with a calm, knowing expression on his face. "Scared?" he asked.

Ena was instantly incensed. "No, I'm not scared," she snapped indignantly.

"Good," he concluded, "then you can go." He glanced at his watch. The minutes were ticking away, and he hated arriving late. "I'll be over to the house to pick you up in an hour. Is that enough time, or do you need more to get ready?"

She didn't know what sort of women he was used to, but she certainly didn't need an hour to get dressed. "I don't need more time—"

He cut her off. "Great, then I'll be there sooner," Mitch told her. He started to leave the corral, then stopped and looked over his shoulder. "You're not walking," he observed. Instead of asking her why, he offered, "I can take you back to the ranch house on my horse."

Ena sighed and finally walked out of the corral. Then with a determined gait, she walked right past him.

"Guess we don't need the horse," he said, addressing Ena's back.

Ena didn't turn around to answer him. All things considered, she felt it was better that way.

* * *

"Wow, I forgot how well you clean up," Mitch said when, true to his word, he arrived at the ranch house less than an hour later to pick her up. Felicity had opened the door to admit him in.

"If that's your idea of a compliment, I think you need to work on your technique," Ena told him, trying very hard not to let him see that his reaction had secretly pleased her.

He nodded solemnly.

"Duly noted," Mitch responded. "But just so you know, that did come from the heart." His eyes swept over the deep blue dress, appreciating the way it clung to her curves—just the way he would have liked to if things were different. "Maybe I should bring my gun with me," he debated.

Ena picked up the shawl she was bringing with her. She had found it earlier in the recesses of her closet. She had forgotten to pack the shawl and take it with her when she'd left ten years ago. The shawl had belonged to her mother. A bittersweet feeling had filled her when she had thrown the shawl over her shoulders and looked herself over in the mirror earlier. She'd come very close to crying.

"Why?" she asked Mitch, now puzzled by his desire to bring a weapon with him. Forever was nothing if not peaceful.

His grin told her the answer was self-explanatory, but he indulged her anyway. "To make sure that nobody gets any ideas about getting you to spend your time exclusively with them." His eyes swept over her again. "You are really something in that dress," he told her.

Ena looked at him for a long moment. And then she

nodded at his compliment. "I guess that's an improve-ment—as long as you don't wind up shooting anyone."

"Only if I have to," Mitch deadpanned. And then he smiled at her and, his voice softening, said, "You do look really nice."

"Thank you. So do you," she told him, returning the compliment.

Mitch's smile deepened, causing two dimples to ap-pear in his cheeks and turning his rugged face into a boyish one.

"Thanks," he told her. Then he added, "Let's just say you bring out the best in me."

With that, he presented his elbow to her.

Ena was tempted to ask if he thought she was going to trip over something, but she refrained. This wasn't the time to be flippant or act independent. Instead, she quietly slipped her arm through his.

"Well, don't you two look pretty," Wade declared with a wide grin when he saw them leaving the house and walking toward Mitch's freshly washed truck.

Mitch didn't rise to the bait. "You're just jealous," he told the wrangler he considered his right-hand man.

"Yeah, I am," Wade admitted. He never took his eyes off Ena. "You look nice, boss." This time his words were directed toward Ena.

She smiled at him. "Thank you," she murmured.

"Get back to work," Mitch told the other man, pre-tending to be stern. And then he winked at the ranch hand. Wade nodded, then went back to the corral.

Helping her into the passenger side of his truck, Mitch took Ena's hand in his. He looked at her, slightly surprised.

"Your hand's icy." The weather didn't warrant that.

"Are you cold?" he asked. Maybe she needed something more than just that shawl. "I can go back in and—"

She shook her head. "I'm just nervous," she confessed.

So much for getting her something warmer, Mitch thought. Rounding the hood of his truck, he got in on the driver's side.

"Why?" he asked. This wasn't like her, he thought.

She shrugged as he started up the truck. "I haven't seen a lot of these people in ten years. They're probably all going to be judging me when they see me, wondering where I've been and why I wasn't there at my father's funeral."

"No, they won't." He sounded so sure of his answer that, for a second, Ena clung to it. "They'll all be envious that you got to leave Forever and make something of yourself. Truth is," he told her, "a lot of them wanted to do just that, but for one reason or another, they never did. But you're the one who did. You got to live an adventure."

"An adventure, huh?" His description amused her. "Funny, I just thought I didn't have a choice. It was either leave Forever, or slowly die by inches in front of a man who hated me since the day I was born. At least," she said with a deep sigh, "that's what I thought at the time."

He glanced in her direction. "And now?"

She thought of all the things Mitch had told her about her father, about the way the man had claimed to feel toward the end of his life.

"And now I'm not so sure." She took a breath, collecting herself as she looked at him. "Can't you drive this thing any faster?"

"I could," Mitch allowed.

He was driving slowly because he wanted to have more time with Ena. There were always other people— the wranglers, not to mention Felicity—around and they couldn't have these more personal conversations with all those ears listening in. But they were alone now, so she couldn't feel that anyone was eavesdropping on their conversation even if it *did* get personal.

"Then do it," Ena instructed.

Which was her way of saying that she didn't like the way this conversation was going, Mitch thought. Well, at least he had broken some ground. That was good enough for now.

Pressing down on the accelerator, he said, "Yes, ma'am," and they took off, going twice as fast as they had been.

Because Murphy's had more available space than Miss Joan's diner did, Miss Joan had decided to hold the anniversary party for Dan and the medical clinic there. Which was just as well because the party turned out to be a joint venture out of necessity. Miss Joan provided the food and the Murphy brothers provided the liquid libations as well as the entertainment, courtesy of Liam Murphy and his band. A professional musician who had gone on tour more than a few times, Liam, the youngest of the three brothers, still enjoyed performing in his own hometown. And no matter where his tour took him, Liam never felt more appreciated than he did back in Forever, where it had all begun.

"This is nice," Ena had to admit as she and Mitch walked inside Murphy's.

Looking around, she found that she recognized several faces. And then several more.

Everywhere she looked within the packed saloon, she

discovered even more faces that were at least vaguely familiar to her. The nervousness she had managed to disguise began to dissipate in earnest.

And then, suddenly, the crowd parted, shifting to either the right or to the left, creating a space for a rather elegant-looking Miss Joan to make her way over to them.

Ena hardly recognized the woman.

"You got her to come," Miss Joan said to Mitch, sounding genuinely pleased. Her eyes crinkled just a bit as she said, "Nice work."

Mitch nodded, pretending to accept his due. "I only had to handcuff her to the back of the truck for part of the way."

"No, he didn't," Ena protested. Mitch looked so serious she was afraid Miss Joan might believe the fantastic claim.

Miss Joan raised a brow in Ena's direction. "Then he had to do it the whole way?" Miss Joan sounded completely serious. Ena began to vehemently deny the statement—and then she heard Miss Joan's high-pitched laugh. "Just having a little fun with you, dear. Just like you should be having," the woman added. She nodded in approval as Liam and his band started up another number. "Good music," she noted. She turned her hazel eyes back toward Ena standing beside Mitch. "Dance."

It wasn't a suggestion.

Mitch slipped one hand around Ena's waist and wrapped his other one around her hand.

Ena looked at him in surprise. "What are you doing?"

"Just following Miss Joan's orders," he told her. "If we don't," he whispered against her ear, "Miss Joan's liable to take out a gun and start shooting at the floor around our feet the way they used to when they wanted to get someone to dance in those old cowboy movies."

He had to be kidding, Ena thought. "Miss Joan wouldn't do that," she protested.

"Maybe not, but I'm not brave enough to find out," Mitch said as he began to sway with her to the slow song that Liam was playing.

Ena wanted to protest that she didn't want to dance, especially not to a slow song, but she didn't want to cause a scene, either. So dancing with Mitch turned out to be the less problematic of the two alternatives—even if it was so close.

Leaning into him, Ena tried as hard as she could not to let herself enjoy what was happening. But she had to admit that it was really difficult for her to remain aloof. Especially since she really *was* enjoying dancing with Mitch. Enjoying being held by him. With so very little effort, she knew that she could allow herself to get carried away.

She had to remain vigilant, Ena silently told herself. Otherwise, she could easily wind up melting— and people would talk.

"People are watching us," she told Mitch, feeling more than a little self-conscious. But even so, the warm feeling she was experiencing only seemed to increase in scope.

"That's because they're all jealous of me," he told her in an easygoing voice.

"No, they're not," she protested.

"Sure they are," he contradicted. He drew his head back for a moment, his eyes looking into hers. "And why not? I'm dancing with the most beautiful woman here."

She struggled to keep her distance, at least emotionally. "I had no idea you were this smooth," she told him.

"If you're referring to my dancing, I've been practic-ing," Mitch admitted. And then he added, "With Felicity."

"I wasn't talking about your dancing technique, I was referring to your tongue," she clarified.

"Oh. Well, what can I say? You inspire me," he re-plied.

Despite trying to maintain an emotional distance between them, she couldn't help laughing.

"What's so funny?" he asked.

"Back in high school, you just kept to yourself. I tried to get your attention a few times," she admitted. "But you always acted like I didn't exist."

"I told you," he reminded her. "I knew that you ex-isted. I also knew that your father existed, and if I made one move on you, just one, I knew that man would skin me alive."

She shook her head. He couldn't have believed that. "You could have made all the moves you wanted. My father wouldn't have cared."

"Just because he never said it out loud didn't mean that he didn't care," Mitch told her. "All you had to do was look into that man's eyes and you knew that he cared. A lot."

He was just trying to make her feel better, she thought. But he couldn't because she knew the truth about the situation.

"Yeah, right." The two words fairly dripped with sarcasm.

"Trust me," he assured her. "It's a guy thing. One guy knows what another one feels. And that man cared," Mitch told her. "He just didn't know how to let you know that."

They would just go round and round about this and not get anywhere. She wanted to drop the subject—

permanently. "I don't feel like talking about my father," she told him, laying her head on Mitch's shoulder as the band started to play another song.

Mitch felt all the powerful emotions he was trying so hard to keep under lock and key struggling against their restraints. For now, he would just focus on holding her and nothing more.

"I never said a word," he told her.

Taking a breath, he found himself breathing in the scent of her hair.

Careful, he warned himself. It was all too easy to get carried away. All it took was one misstep on his part and he could wind up regretting it forever if he scared her off.

It was an evening Mitch didn't want to see end, but perforce, it had to.

But not before he had managed, with Miss Joan's help, to get Ena together with A.J. Prescott, the bank's manager.

More than anything, when Miss Joan brought the man over, Ena just wanted to turn around and run. Dozens of reasons why she shouldn't have this impromptu "meeting" popped up in her head.

However, sensing that it was a now-or-never situation, Ena knew she had to plead her case with Prescott since it was his bank that held the mortgage note on the Double E Ranch.

Keeping in mind what Mitch had told her, that the bank preferred not to foreclose on properties but have them be productive moneymakers, Ena sucked up her courage and laid out her plan on how to make the horse ranch more profitable.

Somewhere along the line, as she talked almost nonstop to the manager, she also brought up the "miracle cure" for migraines by Mitch's mother. When Prescott looked intrigued, she proposed a side business in which she and Mitch could sell the homemade product, comprised of natural ingredients that had already individually been approved by the FDA. She was certain that people would react to the product the way she had. The added proposed sales would be enough to put them over the top as far as being able to keep the ranch running and in the black.

All she needed was for the bank to approve an extension.

Prescott remained quiet for a very long moment. Then, looking over toward Miss Joan, who was standing several feet away from Ena, he finally nodded.

"Considering your father's long-term history with our bank, I'm sure that we will be able to arrange what we call a good faith extension. I'll have McGreevy, our loan officer, draw up the terms and you can look them over. If you find them satisfactory, you can sign the document and keep the ranch. You're better suited to ranching than the bank is," Prescott told her with a smile.

"That's enough business talk for now," Miss Joan declared, coming in between Ena and the manager. "Have some more apple pie, A.J.," Miss Joan suggested. "And you, I believe you owe that studly foreman of yours another dance. Go, dance with him before I do," she urged, putting her hand to Ena's back and pushing her in Mitch's direction.

Ena smiled, feeling both empowered and giddy at the same time because of what had just transpired in the saloon.

"Yes, ma'am," she told Miss Joan as she went to do as the woman advised.

Chapter Seventeen

"You know, for someone who dug in her heels about attending that little shindig today, you wound up practically closing the place down," Mitch laughed as he drove them back to the Double E Ranch. The last time he had looked at his watch, it was almost eleven thirty.

She pretended to frown at him. "Don't lecture me, Parnell. This is the first time I've felt this kind of relief in a long time. I guess I just lost track of time," she confessed.

"Hey, this isn't a lecture," he protested. "I know better than anyone how hard you've been working since you got here. Don't forget, I was the one who suggested that you come to this thing in the first place and blow off some steam," Mitch reminded her.

She hadn't meant to sound as if she was blaming him. "I wound up doing more than that, thanks to you and Miss Joan," she told him. The truth of it was things had gone so well she felt as if she were flying. "It looks like we're going to be getting that extension on the ranch's loan."

He had been standing to the side at the time, acutely aware of everything that was happening because he was so in tune to her body language. He smiled at her now. "You're the one responsible for that, Ena. We had nothing to do with it."

He was the one who had given her the courage to step up and make her pitch to Prescott, not to mention that if it weren't for him, she wouldn't have thought up her strategy with his mother's migraine cure.

"You're the one who got the ball rolling," she pointed out.

"And you're the one who knocked that ball out of the park," he stressed, picking up on her metaphor as he brought his truck to a stop in front of the house. He got out, rounded the truck's hood and came up to the passenger side. "End of the line, boss lady," he said, opening the door for her.

Ena took his hand and got out. "I don't want this day to be over yet," she told him. "Would you like to come inside for a drink?"

She'd already had a couple after her business with Prescott had concluded and Mitch wasn't certain how well she held her liquor. He didn't want alcohol to be the reason things got out of hand.

"Are you sure that's such a good idea?" he asked, bringing her to her door.

Her lips quirked in a bemused smile. "Are you accusing me of trying to get you drunk so I can have my way with you?"

He wasn't sure if she was serious, but he took no

chances. "No, I didn't mean that. I just thought that you might—"

Ena laughed, unlocking the front door. "Relax, Parnell, I'm just kidding. And you don't have to worry about me, either. The one thing I *did* inherit from my father is his ability to hold his liquor. It would take a lot more than two drinks to have any sort of effect on me."

"What would three drinks do?"

"Might make me smile wider," she answered with a wink.

Maybe it was okay to come in for that drink, Mitch decided. "I'd like to see that," he told her. "Okay, you talked me into it," he said, following her inside. "Just remember, this was your idea."

"Funny, I seem to remember that this was yours," she said innocently, closing the front door behind him.

"I don't mean going to the celebration in the first place," Mitch told her. "I'm talking about having a nightcap."

Turning on the light beside the door, Ena crossed to where she knew her father used to keep the liquor. There were still a couple of bottles in the cabinet.

"Less talking, more doing," she said, taking out a half-filled bottle of Wild Turkey whiskey. There were a few mismatched glasses on the counter; she selected two.

"You know, someone else might point out that that's a really loaded statement," Mitch said as he watched her fill two glasses halfway with the amber liquid.

"Someone else?" she echoed, handing him his glass. "But not you?"

He accepted the glass from her and took a sip just to strengthen his resolve. Maybe it was just his imagination, but she looked even more desirable than usual in the low light.

The liquid coursed through his veins, doing little to subdue what was going on inside of him.

His eyes met hers and he could feel his pulse quicken. "You're making it really hard for me to remember my place, boss lady."

Ena shifted. She was only inches away from him. There was just enough space for a breath of air to come between them.

And then even that space was gone.

She had yet to take a sip of her drink. Instead, she raised her eyes to his. "And just what is your place, Mitch?"

Her low voice instantly undulated all along his skin.

"Back in the bunkhouse." He nodded vaguely in the general direction.

"But you're not back in the bunkhouse right now," she pointed out quietly. "You're here, with me."

Heaven help him, good intentions or not, he was really losing ground here, not to mention he was also losing his resolve. The only way he had a chance of doing the right thing was to say something clumsy and crass to her to make her back off.

"Are you trying to seduce me, boss lady?" he asked her.

Rather than take offense, or back off the way he thought she would, Ena merely asked him, "What makes you think that?"

"Every fiber of my being," he answered. Mitch was really struggling now not to just grab hold of Ena and pull her into his arms, giving in to the waves of desire that were insisting on persistently washing over him and drenching him.

Damn, he should have stayed firm and not come in, he thought. Instead, all he could focus on now were her lips as she spoke to him, drawing him in further and further.

"So what's stopping you?" Ena asked.

He was brutally honest in his response. "My sense of self-preservation."

Ena rose on her toes, her tantalizing mouth within an inch of his. "I'm not planning on destroying you," she whispered.

He could feel her breath on his skin, could feel himself weakening as desire blossomed full bore within him, growing so quickly in proportion that it stunned him even as it took him prisoner.

"You might not be planning on it," he told her, his throat growing dry, "but that doesn't mean it's not going to happen."

She turned the tables on him and said the one word that he had said to her when he was trying to get her to attend the party earlier.

"Scared?"

His answer wasn't the one she was expecting. "Terrified," he confessed.

She wasn't sure she understood. "Of me?" she asked in disbelief.

"No, of me," he told her. He curled his fingers into his hands. "If I let go right now, I'm not sure if I can stop myself. Or even manage to hold myself in check."

Ena put her hand on his chest. Warmth instantly generated from the points of contact. "What if I told you that I'm not afraid?"

"I'd tell you that you should be." He said the words so quietly they sounded more like an invitation than a reason for her to flee.

"Let me be the judge of that," she told him, her lips so close to his now that he could almost taste the words as she uttered them.

And that finally did it. Mitch lost what little control he was trying so desperately to hang on to.

The next second, he was no longer attempting to block his urges. Instead, he pulled Ena to him, his arms wrapping around her as he lowered his mouth to hers.

And then he did what he'd been wanting to do since the very first moment he had laid eyes on her back in high school, more than ten years ago.

He kissed her.

His kiss deepened to the point that he lost all concept of anything beyond the small circle that the two of them created. Lost himself in the taste, the feel, the very scent of her.

This was exactly the way she had imagined it would be, Ena thought as her heart leaped up.

Better.

The delicious taste of his lips against hers reduced her to a mass of swirling, molten desire.

Her arms went around his neck and she completely lost herself in him, experiencing not just the rush of desire but all the vast cravings and appetites that were created in its wake.

She couldn't remember the last time she had even had any time to enjoy the company of a man in her life, much less want to make love with him the way she now ached to do with Mitch. Work had always seemed so much more important to her than just a passing dalliance.

But that was because none of the men she had encountered while building up her professional life had ever been anything like Mitch.

There was something about Mitch that made her want to break all the rules she had set for herself and not give a damn that they were being broken.

Technically she was his boss, but she didn't want Mitch to think of her that way now. She just wanted them to be on the same equal footing for one precious evening.

She wanted to make love with him—and to have him want to make love with her, as well as *to* her.

Suddenly, Ena felt herself tottering on the brink of disappointment when Mitch drew his head back and looked at her.

"Are you sure about this?" he asked.

"Are you having second thoughts?" she heard herself asking. Maybe he didn't find her desirable and here she was, forcing herself on him. The thought stung more than she would have imagined.

She had no idea how to pull out of this tailspin that was about to claim her.

And then Mitch said, "Oh, Lord, no. You're a beautiful, desirable woman and no sane man would want to step away from you, much less have second thoughts about what's happening here. But I don't want you getting the wrong idea," he told her, even though just voicing those words cost him, because more than anything in the world, he didn't want her pulling away from him.

Ena's heart was racing so fast she thought it was going to break her ribs and leap out of her chest. She also knew that she was in danger of totally crumbling if he stopped what was about to happen right now.

"What's the right idea?" she asked in a barely audible whisper.

Oh, to hell with it, he thought. He'd done his best to be noble but he was only human. "The right idea is that

I'm having trouble keeping my hands off you because I've had fantasies about you from the very first time I saw you." Then, to prove that this wasn't just a line, he told her exactly when that was. "February 6, second-period English class."

And just like that, Ena melted. "Damn," she murmured, "you couldn't have said anything sexier if you tried."

His eyes crinkled as he smiled at her. "Guess I'm doomed."

Ena threaded her arms around his neck again and smiled up into his eyes. "Guess you are."

This time when their lips met, she secretly marveled that something akin to a spontaneous combustion didn't occur. There was certainly enough heat being generated between them to cause it.

She felt his lips slip down her throat, then press warm kisses along first one side of her neck, then the other, creating all sorts of havoc within her stomach and limbs.

Lost in the sensations he was creating, she reached for the buttons of his shirt, but Mitch shifted and suddenly, she felt herself being swept up into his arms. He started walking.

Dazed, confused, she looked at him.

"Felicity might come down for a midnight snack," he told her, heading toward the stairs. "We wouldn't want to broaden her *education*," he warned.

Ena suppressed a giggle.

She realized Mitch was taking her up to her room. Her excitement increased twofold as anticipation of what was to come once her door was closed took hold of her.

She managed to keep herself in check until Mitch

reached the landing. The moment he did, she let her ardor loose.

He had to stop walking for a second as her hot kisses landed on his face, his neck, the lobes of his ears, everywhere she could reach.

The sound of his increasingly heavier breathing told her that she was getting to him, which in turn made her even more excited.

"You are driving me totally crazy," he gasped, trying to catch his breath. His arms tightened around her to avoid dropping her, but, he discovered, it wasn't easy maintaining his hold on her.

The second they were in her room and he had closed the door with his elbow, he crossed to her bed and laid her down. The next second, he joined her, hardly breaking their contact for more than a fraction of a second.

He eagerly undid the zipper at her back, then tugged at the material, sliding her dress down the curves of her body until it was just a discarded scrap of material on the floor.

He couldn't take his eyes off her.

"You're overdressed," she breathed, tugging on his belt and the shirt he had tucked in beneath it.

"I am," he agreed, or at least thought he did. His head was spinning, intoxicated by her to the point that down was up, and up was down, and anything beyond the bed didn't exist. He didn't know if he said the words out loud or only thought them.

All he knew was that he wanted her.

His fingers flew over the buttons of his shirt, undoing whatever she hadn't already opened. He pulled off his boots in what seemed like one uninterrupted movement. His jeans quickly followed his boots, leaving him only wearing one last small article of material.

And then it was her turn again.

Mitch swiftly removed her bra and underwear in what seemed like one fluid motion.

His eyes devoured her. "You're so beautiful it hurts."

"Now that," she murmured as she linked her arms around his neck again and brought him down to her, "is a compliment."

She could almost feel his smile as it spread along his lips. "Glad you approve."

"I do. I do," she declared before she sealed her mouth to his again.

They melded, a tangle of arms and legs and sealed hot body parts, rolling around on the bed and reveling in the sizzling press of two bodies searching for at least a temporary moment of salvation.

He surprised her by *not* immediately taking her. Instead, Mitch further impressed her by showing her how patient he could be. He made love to her by degrees, kissing her over and over again, priming her body for the final ultimate moment.

Mitch artfully heightened her anticipation until she was certain she was going to explode waiting for him to make them one single unit.

Just as she was about to take the lead because she couldn't wait any longer, Mitch was suddenly right over her. He was balancing his weight on his elbows. Then, his eyes on hers, he parted her legs with his knee.

Her breath caught in her throat as he entered her, her heart all but slamming against her rib cage. The next moment, he began to move, slowly, deliberately, each pass increasing in rhythm and speed.

He was going faster and faster. Ena found herself racing with him, determined to reach that final pinnacle when he did. And when they reached it, the explosion shuddered through their bodies. A feeling of joy all but drenched her. The sensation was so much more intense than anything she might have anticipated.

Her arms tightened around Mitch as he held tightly on to her.

She felt his smile against her neck as he slowly descended back to earth, reaching it at the exact same moment that she did.

She didn't want to move. Instead, she just wanted to savor the moment and pretend that it was never going to end.

Even though she knew it would, all too soon.

Chapter Eighteen

Mitch shifted his body, moving to the side so that his weight was no longer on Ena. Propping himself up on his elbow, he smiled at her.

"You were magnificent," he said, his voice caressing her.

"Funny, I was going to say the same thing to you," Ena teased.

Mitch gently brushed his fingers through her hair lightly framing her face. "I was inspired."

Ena raised her eyebrow, amused. "Oh?"

He heard the mischief in her voice and grinned as he drew her closer. "Give me a couple of minutes and I'm sure I'll be inspired again," he promised.

"A couple of minutes?" Ena questioned. "That seems like a long time," she commented, punctuating each and every word with a kiss.

"You've got to remember," he told her with breathless effort, "that you took a lot out of me."

"I know," she said, her eyes crinkling as she continued kissing him between each word she uttered. Pausing for a second to look into his eyes, she resumed pressing kisses to his face and throat. "And I loved every minute of it."

His resistance evaporating, Mitch took hold of her, pulling Ena on top of him. The next second, without any warning, he suddenly reversed their positions so that she was beneath him.

"No more than I did, Ena," he assured her.

And then there was no more talking. Instead, he lost himself in her, taking her back across the wild, passionate terrain they had already crossed only a few memorable moments ago.

Ena slipped into the warm, welcoming embrace that lovemaking created, reveling in the way being with Mitch like this made her feel.

Ena blinked, trying to focus her mind and her eyes as she slowly woke up. Moving her shoulders against the mattress, she stretched, doing her best to come to.

When she did, she realized that the space beside her was empty.

Mitch was gone.

Well, what did you expect? That he was going to serenade you with banjo music the second you opened your eyes? You had a great night, but now it's back to normal, she told herself.

Now the best thing that she could do was to *act* normal. No muss, no fuss and definitely not anything that would make anyone else suspect that they had spent the night together.

Throwing the covers aside, she got up and quickly got ready, telling herself over and over that this was just another day on the ranch and that there was work that needed to be done.

Work, Ena reminded herself, that now *could* be done because she had managed to get the bank to grant them that much-needed extension.

She caught herself humming as she went downstairs.

"Well, you certainly look happy," Felicity said, greeting her when Ena walked into the kitchen. The woman's dark eyes swept over her. "Did you have a good night?" the housekeeper asked.

Ena had no idea if Felicity was making idle conversation or if the housekeeper had somehow sensed what had happened between Mitch and her last night and the woman was making a general comment on it.

Hoping it was the former, Ena decided to throw a few specifics into her answer. "The party at Murphy's was very lively, so yes, I had a very good time."

The knowing look in Felicity's dark eyes told her the housekeeper wasn't really referring to that, but at least for now, to keep things simple, Ena decided that was her story and she was sticking to it.

"By the way," Ena said innocently, "did Mitch come by already?"

Felicity shook her head. "No, I did not see Mr. Mitch. He and the caballeros are working as usual." Making something on the stove, she briefly glanced in Ena's direction. "Horses need to be fed and groomed. They do not care if it is the weekend or not."

"Very true," Ena agreed. She picked up a piece of bread to put into the toaster. "I'll just grab a piece of toast," she told the woman.

Felicity turned from the stove and gave her a very frosty eye.

"No, you will sit down and have breakfast like a

civilized person. Engines do not run on air. They need fuel," the housekeeper declared, leaving absolutely no room for argument.

Ena didn't even have to think about it. "Okay, I'll have breakfast," she said, surrendering.

She felt too good to get into an argument with the woman—all she wanted to do was be able to get out and find Mitch as quickly as possible—not to say anything in particular, just to prove to herself that last night had really happened.

Felicity set the plate down in front of Ena and then stepped back as the latter began to eat. The woman's thin lips puckered into a disapproving frown.

"You are not a vacuum cleaner," Felicity said sharply. "You are supposed to chew your food, not gulp it down in a chunk."

"I am chewing," Ena told the housekeeper, consuming the food the woman had placed in front of her as quickly as possible.

Felicity crossed her arms before her, a monument of disapproval. "Do not blame me if you wind up getting sick," she said.

"I wouldn't dare," Ena murmured under her breath.

Finished, she pushed the plate away from her and got to her feet.

"Thank you," she called out to the housekeeper as she hurried to the door.

Felicity shook her head again, following Ena to the front door.

"A woman is always supposed to keep a man waiting," the housekeeper informed her. But Felicity knew that she was wasting her breath, addressing the air. Ena was already gone.

Even though she had hurried out, Ena heard what

Felicity had said. To be honest, part of her agreed with the housekeeper. That was how the game was usually played, at least in the beginning.

But she didn't want to play any games. She never had. What she wanted was to be able to enjoy Mitch and his company for as long as possible, especially since in her heart of hearts she knew she was supposed to be on a schedule.

She was fairly certain that was how Mitch saw it. He probably assumed that in six months—less now because she'd already put in some time—she would go back to her world. Depending on the situation, she would have either sold the ranch to someone local or, more likely, kept the ranch herself. In that case she would have Mitch run the place for her while she went back to Dallas to do what she did best: work with numbers.

The moment she laid out her plan for her herself, she suddenly realized that she really wasn't as sure about it as she had initially been. Ten years ago she had thought that she wanted to get as far away from ranching as she could. Her goal all along had been to prove to her late father, looking up—or down—from whatever vantage point his life had placed him in, that she was up to the challenge he had laid down for her.

Once that was done, she would go back to life the way it had been.

Except the idea of resuming the life she had had just a little while ago was not as pleasing to her as she had once thought. But that didn't change the fact that she assumed Mitch still thought that she was leaving the moment the six months were up.

Maybe that was why he'd felt free to fool around with her the way he had. Because, from that perspective, there were no strings attached to what they had done, no promises made in the heat of passion that needed to be kept. Last night had been about two consenting adults enjoying one another.

Except that she suspected one of the adults had enjoyed what happened last night a little more than the other had.

And if Mitch became even the slightest bit aware of that, she felt in her heart that it could very well scare him away.

Which meant that she had to keep a lid on things no matter how tempted she might be to say something, Ena firmly told herself.

But it definitely wasn't going to be easy. Ena could feel her heart leaping up the second that she saw him.

For his part, Mitch saw her coming from half a field away. He was grateful he had that much time to steel himself off.

He was certain that Ena wouldn't want anyone else to know about their night together, as magnificent as it had been. After all, she was the owner here and he was, at bottom, just a hired hand. The last thing he wanted was for her to get the impression that he had made love with her thinking that would give him some sort of advantage or even leverage over her.

But damn, just watching her walking toward him had him feeling things, stirring up his insides. It had him wishing that he had spent more time perfecting a poker face.

When she reached the area where he and the others were, Mitch touched the brim of his Stetson as if to tip it to her. "Morning, Miss O'Rourke. Wasn't sure if you'd be joining us this morning," he told her.

"Morning," Ena echoed. "Why wouldn't I?" she challenged. "Horses don't care if it's Sunday." She looked at the horseshoes that were piled up on the ground. "What are you doing?" she asked, directing her eyes as well as her question toward the other wranglers more than Mitch.

"We're shoeing some of the new foals," Wade told her, nodding toward a heavyset wrangler who had on a black leather apron. Ena assumed he was the blacksmith. "The ones that are fully grown," Wade added. "We thought if you sold them at auction that would bring in enough money to keep the ranch going awhile longer."

That surprised her. "You didn't tell them?" she asked, looking at Mitch.

Mitch merely smiled in response. "I figured it was your news to tell."

She would have thought that those would be the first words out of his mouth the second he gathered the other wranglers around him this morning before they started working.

"Tell us what?" Billy asked, looking from Ena to Mitch.

"Go ahead," Mitch urged, nodding at her.

"We saw the bank manager at Murphy's last night—" she began.

"*Miss O'Rourke* saw the bank manager," Mitch corrected.

She just continued as if he hadn't said anything, "And the man agreed to extend the note on the ranch as long as we start showing a profit."

She decided to keep the details about the herbal cure

by Mitch's mother to herself for the time being. It was enough that Mitch knew what she was planning to do with it—and why.

"Can we?" Wade asked, directing the question to Mitch.

Mitch in turn looked at Ena, redirecting the question to her. "I think we can," she said with confidence.

"All right, men, you heard the boss lady. Now, get back to work," Mitch ordered.

As if on cue, activity restarted all around him.

Ena stood off to the extreme right as a number of the wranglers took charge of several of the horses, leading them to a fenced-off area to await being shod. A few of the horses were skittish and had to be calmed.

Mitch has called her *boss lady*, she thought. Was that for the men's benefit, or did he actually think of her that way himself? If he did, then they couldn't really be on equal footing, Ena thought. She didn't want that. She didn't want him feeling that she was above him. That would adversely affect their relationship.

But maybe Mitch didn't think of them as having a relationship, she thought, her stomach twisting as the possibility occurred to her. Maybe it really was just about a good time for him and nothing more.

It should be that way for you, she silently insisted. *It's about time you loosened up.*

She'd never had the sort of wild, carefree adolescence the way she knew that a lot of others had had. She'd been too busy toeing a line once her mother was gone. And after that, once she left home, she had been too busy trying to create a life for herself. Somehow, there had never really been any time to just be young, to explore her own feminine wiles.

Was this how it went between men and women? A

good time was had without any promises of something more? She honestly didn't know. She had never had anyone for guidance when it came to this, no one to look to as a role model.

Her mother, whom she adored, had never taught her anything except how to defer to her father. There had to be more to a relationship than that.

But maybe she was expecting too much from Mitch. Maybe he was just in it for the fun of it and not anything else.

Okay, she decided, she could do that. She could just ride this wave and see where it would take her, enjoying this exhilarating ride for as long as it continued, Ena told herself.

Their eyes met for a second and then Mitch crossed over to her. He didn't want Ena to feel that he was presuming too much, or that he felt that last night had given him a special status with her because he knew that it hadn't.

Still, he didn't just want to leave it at that without saying a word, or worse, pretending that last night hadn't happened. Because it had. It had been glorious, lighting up his life the way it had never been lit before.

He had deliberately left her bedroom while she was sleeping this morning because if he had stayed, he knew he would have been tempted to make love with her all over again. And while they had made love twice the night before, there was something about daylight that forced things into perspective. The last thing he wanted was for her to feel pressured. Nor did he want her to reject him. He really didn't know how he would be able to deal with that.

But there was certainly nothing wrong with his coming up to her at the start of a new day and asking, "How are you feeling?"

That had come out of the blue, Ena thought. Rather than give him a glib answer, she asked in a quiet voice, "About?"

Mitch shrugged vaguely. "Everything," he said, feeling that it was best not to cite anything in particular.

She flashed a noncommittal smile. "I'm feeling just fine."

Maybe he shouldn't have said anything, he thought. "Good. Me, too."

Talk about vague, Ena thought. They could be discussing their feelings about the price of grain or the state of the weather. Was he being vague like this to protect her or himself?

She didn't have a clue. She knew what she wanted him to be saying and doing, but only if *he* wanted to, not because she did.

Ena took a breath. She needed to sort all this out for herself, calmly and rationally. And then, and only then, would she be able to come to Mitch and have that conversation that she felt they both needed to have.

Because being vague like this actually made her feel trapped in limbo.

"You sure you're okay?" he asked her, keeping his own voice low.

"Yes," she answered crisply, her eyes meeting his. "I'm sure."

"Then I'm going to get back to work," Mitch told her. He turned on his heel and went walking back to his men.

She watched as Mitch took measured steps away from her. She couldn't help wondering if the man was aware that his hips moved ever so temptingly with each step that he took.

She found herself suddenly reliving last night. Ena promised herself that she wasn't going to allow what had sprung to life between them to be over, no matter what it took.

Like a flower in the desert, it needed to be watered and nurtured and she intended to do both.

Chapter Nineteen

Well, it was official, Ena thought. It was more than three weeks since she and Mitch had made love. More than three weeks since he had so much as even touched her in a chaste, impartial way.

At this point she was struggling not to let anger get the better of her because she could now add the term *one-night stand* to her dating resume.

There was no other way to describe what had happened between her and Mitch, because ever since that one glorious, delicious night, the ranch foreman hadn't even tried to hold her hand—or any other part of her for that matter.

Ena felt let down and hurt, and had no idea what to make of it because she had never been in this position before.

It certainly didn't help that Mitch acted as if nothing out of the ordinary had happened between them. The way he behaved—since that night—anyone watching him would have said that they were nothing more than two people working on a horse ranch together.

In the beginning, she thought she had done something wrong. After a while, though, she decided that *he* was the one to blame. So when Mitch spoke to her, she did her best to give him a frosty shoulder.

But that gave her no satisfaction. With each passing day, more and more she felt as if she were drowning in a barrel filled with ice water. Drowning and without a single clue how to save herself.

If something didn't happen soon, she knew she was going to go down for the third and final time.

Each day she got up and went through the motions of working on the ranch, while deep within, she felt as if her heart were breaking apart. It was an effort to try to keep her mind on what she was doing.

And then, just when she felt as if she had reached a crossroads, she saw Cash pulling up in front of the ranch house in his car.

Standing close by, Mitch saw the lawyer's car, too. "Wonder what this is all about," he said.

Seeing the car, Ena's first thought was that Cash had found an addendum to her father's will. The way her luck was going, there were probably more hoops for her to jump through before she could finally become the sole owner of the Double E.

When she didn't say anything in response to his question, Mitch asked her point-blank, "Trouble?"

Ena didn't even look his way. She had to harden her heart when it came to this man and it had to start now.

"Nothing that would concern you," she retorted, walking toward Cash's vehicle.

"Ouch," Wade said, overhearing. "That one drew blood." He looked at Mitch. "You two doing okay?"

The answer to that was obvious. "Don't you have work to do?" Mitch asked.

Wade had always known when to step back. "Absolutely," he said to the foreman and began to move toward the corral.

Mitch stood where he was for a minute, then decided that if the lawyer was here because of something that had to do with the ranch, as foreman he would hear about it sooner or later, so it might as well be sooner rather than later. With that thought in mind, he crossed quickly toward Ena and the lawyer. The latter had just gotten out of his vehicle.

Mitch got there in time to hear Ena ask, "What brings you here, Cash?"

"Good news. Possibly," Cash qualified. "That's why I wanted to deliver it to you in person."

Because of the way things had been going, her patience was at a low point. "Well, what is it?" she pressed. "My orchestra has the day off, otherwise I would have already signaled for a drumroll," she told him. Then she immediately said, "I'm sorry. I'm afraid I'm a little testy lately."

"Well, this just might make you less testy," Cash told her with an encouraging smile. "You have an offer to buy the ranch."

"An offer?" she asked, confused. "But I haven't put up the ranch for sale."

"No, but Edward Larabee seemed pretty eager to annex this ranch to make it part of his spread. It seems that he sees himself as being at the head of a horse empire. Someone must have told him that you're not all that thrilled to be back here ranching," Cash speculated.

Ena was acutely aware that Mitch was standing there, taking all this in. That made her even more uncomfortable. "Well, in any case, I can't sell the Double E to him yet. You know that." She pressed her lips together, feeling trapped. "The terms were that I had to stay and work the ranch for six months," she reminded him needlessly.

Cash nodded. "Larabee's aware of that. He's more than willing to wait, as long as when you are ready to sell, you consider his offer before the others."

"Others?" Mitch asked, surprised. "There are others?"

"No, not yet," Cash said. "But once word gets around that the Double E is for sale, there might be others." Cash reconsidered his statement. "As a matter of fact, there most likely will be. I just wanted to come out and let you know about this in case you've started feeling like you're going to be trapped here."

She didn't want that getting around. "I never said I felt trapped," she protested.

Until she had arrived back in Forever, she had been very careful about keeping all her personal feelings to herself.

"You didn't have to," Cash told her kindly. "It was there, in your eyes, for anyone to see." He could tell that wasn't what she wanted to hear. He decided that it was best to wind this up. "Anyway, Larabee wants to be first in line when your required six months are up." He glanced at his watch. "I've got to be getting back."

As he got into his car, he said, "Congratulations. This is good news, I hope." Then, starting up the engine, he drove away.

"Larabee's got a hell of a nerve, making that offer," Mitch said as he watched Cash's car disappear down the road.

"Why would you say that?" Ena challenged.

"Why?" he echoed, wondering why she sounded so irritated. "Because you're not going to sell."

She gave him a withering look. "I'm not?"

"No," Mitch declared. And then he looked at her face more closely and realized that maybe he was taking things for granted. "Are you?"

Ena shrugged. "It's definitely worth thinking about," she answered. "I mean, there's really nothing to keep me here."

"Nothing to keep you here?" he repeated, stunned. She wasn't serious, was she? "You were *born* here."

Ena tossed her head, dismissing his argument. "That's not enough of a reason to keep me here."

He stared at her, completely confused. "I don't understand," he said. "I thought when you convinced Prescott to extend the loan on the ranch—and he agreed," Mitch stressed, "that you'd made your mind up to stay here and run the place."

Shrugging, Ena turned away and began to head to the house. "Not everything is what it seems," she informed him coldly.

That just succeeded in making him even more confused. "What's *that* supposed to mean?"

She didn't bother turning around. "Whatever you want it to."

She was almost at the house when she heard Mitch call after her.

"Bruce'll miss you."

That stopped her for half a second. "He'll get over it," she said, continuing toward the front door.

Mitch stood there, feeling something crumble inside him with each step she took. For one long moment, he debated letting her go, but then something urged him not to, to give this "thing" between them—whatever it

was—one last shot despite all his noble attempts at re-
straint to the contrary.

Ena had reached the house and walked in through
the door, afraid that she would break down before she
got inside. She had taken two steps into the house when
the door behind her flew open again.

"No, he won't," Mitch declared. "And even if he
does—I won't," he said, his voice dropping.

No, she told herself fiercely, she wasn't going to fall
for that again. Mitch's actions spoke louder than his
words and he had practically shunned her these last
three weeks. She let herself fall for him, had given him
her heart and then practically gotten kicked in the teeth
for her stupidity.

Well, not again.

Swinging around, Ena looked at him, her eyes blaz-
ing. "Oh, I'm sure you'll get over it in record time. As
a matter of fact, I bet that you probably already have."

He stared at her, lost. "What are you talking about?"

"I'm talking about you acting as if I had leprosy."
To underscore her words, she hit him in the chest with
the flat of her hand. "As if I was someone you had to
endure in order to keep your job."

When she went to hit him again, he took a step back,
catching her hand before she could make contact. "Still
don't understand," he said pointedly.

"Then think about it!" she all but shouted in his face.
"We made love, you put another notch in your belt and
then you cut me dead. Seems simple enough to understand to me." Her eyes narrowed, shooting daggers at
him. "Now, if you have nothing else—"

Mitch caught hold of her shoulders to keep her in
place. "I have nothing else if you sell this ranch and
leave Forever."

He was worried about his job, she thought angrily. "Don't worry, I'm sure that Larabee will keep you on as foreman. I can even specify that as being one of my terms when I sell it to him—"

"The hell with being foreman." He blew out a breath as he looked up at the ceiling, searching for words. And then he looked at her. "I gave this my best shot, but I can't do this any longer."

It was her turn not to understand. "I'm sure that I don't know—"

Now that he had found the words, he couldn't allow himself to be distracted. "Don't take this the wrong way, Ena, but shut up."

Startled, she stared at him. "What?"

"Shut up," Mitch repeated. "Do you want to know why I stayed away from you? Because I realized that you might think what happened between us was because I wanted to seal my place on the ranch. That you'd think I wanted to help you run the ranch or maybe even something more than that. But I don't care about the ranch," he insisted, then felt that needed clarification. "I mean, I care about the ranch, but definitely not more than I care about you." He saw the disbelief on her face. He wasn't doing this well, he upbraided himself. "Look, this is a whole new place for me." He shrugged helplessly. "I'm shoeing a horse and seeing your face."

Ena tilted her head. "I'm not sure that's a compliment."

"Well, it is," he insisted, "because nothing has ever interfered with work for me before—until there was you." He knew he was saying too much, but now that he had gotten started, he couldn't stop himself. "I want you so much that I literally *hurt* inside. But what I don't want is you thinking that I'm after the ranch. The only thing I'm after is you." He took in a shaky breath. "I felt that way ever since I saw you in Mrs. Brickman's English class and I feel that way now." His eyes looked into hers. "I just don't know how to prove it to you."

Ena smiled. "You just did."

"What?" He didn't know if she was kidding him or not. "How?"

She supposed it was so simple he didn't see it. "Because you remembered when you first saw me. The thing is, you didn't just make that up because I remember it, too," she told him.

That first time was very important to him. Had it actually been that way for her, too? Or was she just pulling his leg for some reason? "You do?"

She smiled at Mitch. "I do."

His mind began racing, making plans. "Look, maybe I can find some work in Dallas," he began.

She stopped him right there. "Why would you want to do that?"

He told her the truth. "Because the idea of my staying here when you leave makes me feel like my insides are all being scraped out."

She smiled at him. "Your insides are safe, Mitch. I'm not going anywhere."

He didn't understand. Was she having fun at his expense? "But you just said—"

Ena stopped him right there. "I say a lot of things when I'm hurt," she told him.

"Hurt?" he questioned. Was she telling him that he'd managed to hurt her? He'd never even considered that was possible.

Ena closed her eyes for a moment, shaking her head. "You are going to require a lot of patience and work."

Maybe this was going to be all right after all, he

thought. "I'm all yours," he told her. "Do whatever you want with me," Mitch said. "As a matter of fact, I insist on it."

Humor entered her eyes. "Careful what you wish for," she warned.

Now that the barriers were finally down, he felt he could be honest about everything. And it was time he told her. "Do you know what I wanted to say to you the first time I saw you?"

"What?"

"I wanted to say 'Will you marry me?'" He saw her looking at him skeptically. "I didn't," he continued, "because I knew who your father was and I was going to ask him for a job the minute I graduated. I was afraid that if he heard that I'd said that to you, he'd accuse me of just saying that in order to make him consider me for that job."

Ena laughed. Boy, had he been wrong. "You obviously didn't know my father."

"I also wanted to say it that night we came home from Murphy's," he told her. "I didn't say it then because you were so confident that you were going to get that extension from the bank and I didn't want you thinking I was trying to take advantage of the situation, you know, marrying you because of the ranch."

"And you started keeping your distance for the same reason," she guessed.

"It made sense at the time," he said, although hearing it out loud now showed him how foolish he had been.

"If you're given to making stupid decisions," she concluded crisply.

He smiled at her. "That being said, I'm through with making stupid decisions."

She had a feeling that there was more. "All right," she said, encouraging him to continue.

He took a breath. "Now, I don't want you to think that I'm rushing you."

"What am I not being rushed about?" she asked.

He took another breath, a deeper one this time. "I have loved you ever since I first saw you in Mrs. Brickman's English class, and when the dust finally settles, I'd like you to consider..." He tried again. "Do you think that you might be able to consider..."

Ena looked up at him. "Are you asking me to marry you?"

He supposed he *was* making a mess of it, he thought. "I'm trying to."

She cocked her head. "But?"

"I guess what's stopping me is I don't think I can handle you saying no."

Her eyes smiled at him first. "Well, lucky for you, I don't plan on saying no—that is, if you ever finally ask."

"Really?" His smile seemed to grow until it encompassed his entire face.

"First you have to ask," she reminded him.

Then, to her surprise, Mitch took her hand and got down on one knee. "Ena Meredith O'Rourke, will you marry me?"

She winced when he said her full name. "Wait, you *know* my middle name?" she questioned in surprise. It wasn't something that she typically told people. She had never liked the name, even though it had belonged to her parental grandmother.

"I know everything there is to know about you," Mitch told her.

She was beginning to believe that, she thought.

"Well, since you know my middle name, I guess I'm

going to have to marry you." She blinded him with her smile and said, "So, yes! Yes, I will marry you."

That was all he needed to hear. Mitch pulled her into his arms and did what he had longed to do for the last three weeks. He kissed her.

And he kept on kissing her for a very long, long time.

* * * * *

We've got some exciting changes coming in our February 2020 Special Edition books!
Our covers have been redesigned, and the emotional contemporary romances from your favorite authors will be longer in length.

Be sure to come back next month for more great stories from Special Edition!

Don't miss previous romances by Marie Ferrarella, from Harlequin Special Edition:

Bridesmaid for Hire
The Lawman's Romance Lesson
Adding Up to Family
An Engagement for Two

AVAILABLE THIS MONTH FROM
Harlequin® Special Edition

FORTUNE'S FRESH START
The Fortunes of Texas: Rambling Rose • by Michelle Major

In the small Texas burg of Rambling Rose, real estate investor Callum Fortune is making a big splash. The last thing he needs is any personal complications slowing his pace—least of all nurse Becky Averill, a beautiful widow with twin baby girls!

HER RIGHT-HAND COWBOY
Forever, Texas • by Marie Ferrarella

A clause in her father's will requires Ena O'Rourke to work the family ranch for six months before she can sell it. She's livid at her father throwing a wrench in her life from beyond the grave. But Mitch Randall, foreman of the Double E, is always there for her. As Ena spends more time on the ranch—and with Mitch—new memories are laid over the old...and perhaps new opportunities to make a life.

SECOND-CHANCE SWEET SHOP
Wickham Falls Weddings • by Rochelle Alers

Brand-new bakery owner Sasha Manning didn't anticipate that the teenager she hired would have a father more delectable than anything in her shop window! Sasha still smarts from falling for a man too good to be true. Divorced single dad Dwight Adams will have to prove to Sasha that he's the real deal and not a wolf in sheep's clothing... and learn to trust someone with his heart along the way.

COOKING UP ROMANCE
The Taylor Triplets • by Lynne Marshall

Lacy was a redhead with a pink food truck who prepared mouthwatering meals. Hunky construction manager Zack Gardner agreed to let her feed his hungry crew in exchange for cooking lessons for his young daughter. But it looked like the lovely businesswoman was transforming the single dad's life in more ways than one—since a family secret is going to change both of their lives in ways they never expected.

RELUCTANT HOMETOWN HERO
Wildfire Ridge • by Heatherly Bell

Former army officer Ryan Davis doesn't relish the high-profile role of town sheriff, but when duty calls, he responds. Even if it means helping animal rescuer Zoey Castillo find her missing foster dog. When Ryan asks her out, Zoey is wary of a relationship in the spotlight—especially given her past. If the sheriff wants to date her, he'll have to prove that two legs are better than four.

THE WEDDING TRUCE
Something True • by Kerri Carpenter

For the sake of their best friends' wedding, divorce attorney Xander Ryan and wedding planner Grace Harris are calling a truce. Now they must plan the perfect wedding shower together. But Xander doesn't believe in marriage! And Grace believes in romance and true love. Clearly, they have nothing in common. In fact, all Xander feels when Grace is near is disdain and...desire. Wait. What?

**LOOK FOR THESE AND OTHER HARLEQUIN SPECIAL EDITION BOOKS
WHEREVER BOOKS ARE SOLD, INCLUDING MOST BOOKSTORES,
SUPERMARKETS, DISCOUNT STORES AND DRUGSTORES.**

HSEATMBPA0120

COMING NEXT MONTH FROM

(H) HARLEQUIN

SPECIAL EDITION

Available January 21, 2020

#2743 FORTUNE'S TEXAS SURPRISE
The Fortunes of Texas: Rambling Rose • by Stella Bagwell
Until he meets foster mother Stephanie Fortune, rancher Acton Donovan has never pictured himself as a family man. Now suddenly he's thinking about wedding rings and baby cradles! But can he convince himself he's good enough for a woman from the prominent Fortune family?

#2744 FOR THE TWINS' SAKE
Dawson Family Ranch • by Melissa Senate
Bachelor cowboy Noah Dawson finds a newborn on his doorstep with a note that it's his baby, but the infant girl's surprise identity changes his life forever. Now he's reunited with Sara Mayhew, his recently widowed ex-girlfriend, and they're spending Christmas together for the twins' sake—at least, that's what they keep telling themselves...

#2745 A CHANCE FOR THE RANCHER
Match Made in Haven • by Brenda Harlen
Patrick Stafford trades his suit for a Stetson and risks it all on a dude ranch. But it's the local vet, Dr. Brooke Langley, who really challenges him. Is this playboy rancher ready to take a risk on a single mom and become a family man?

#2746 HER HOMECOMING WISH
Gallant Lake Stories • by Jo McNally
Being the proverbial good girl left her brokenhearted and alone. Now Mackenzie Wallace is back and wants excitement with her old crush. She hopes there's still some bad boy lurking beneath the single father's upright exterior. Dan Adams isn't the boy he was—but secrets from his past might still manage to keep them apart.

#2747 DAUGHTER ON HIS DOORSTEP
by Teresa Southwick
When Luke McCoy moved next door, Shelby Richards knew he'd discover the truth. Within minutes, young Emma was on his doorstep, asking Luke if he really was her daddy. Shelby had her reasons, but Luke is not so quick to forgive. And as Shelby saw Luke with their daughter, her heart was not so quick to forget what they'd all missed out on.

#2748 THE BARTENDER'S SECRET
Masterson, Texas • by Caro Carson
Quiet, sheltered, educated, shy Shakespeare professor Delphinia Ray is way out of Connor McClaine's league. So he tries to push her away, convinced she can't handle the harsh truth about his past. But maybe Delphinia is the one to help him face his demons...

YOU CAN FIND MORE INFORMATION ON UPCOMING HARLEQUIN TITLES, FREE EXCERPTS AND MORE AT HARLEQUIN.COM.

HSECNM0120

Mackenzie Wallace is back and wants excitement with her old crush. She hopes there's still some bad boy lurking beneath the single father's upright exterior. Dan Adams isn't the boy he was—but secrets from his past might still manage to keep them apart.

Read on for a sneak preview of the next book in the Gallant Lake Stories series, Her Homecoming Wish, by Jo McNally.

"There's an open bottle of very expensive scotch on the counter, just waiting for someone to enjoy it." She laughed again, softly this time. "And I'd *really* like to hear the story of how Danger Dan turned into a lawman."

Dan grimaced. He hated that stupid nickname Ryan had made up, even if he *had* earned it back then. Especially coming from Mack.

"Is your husband waiting upstairs?" Dan wasn't sure where that question came from, but, to be fair, all Mack had ever talked about was leaving Gallant Lake, having a big wedding and a bigger house. The girl had goals, and from what he'd heard, she'd reached every one of them.

"I don't have a husband anymore." She brushed past him and headed toward the counter. "So are you joining me or not?"

Dan glanced at his watch, not sure how to digest that information. "I'm off duty in fifteen minutes."

Her long hair swung back and forth as she walked ahead of him. So did her hips. *Damn.*

"And you're all about following the rules now? You really have changed, haven't you? Pity. I guess I'm drinking my first glass alone. You'll just have to catch up."

He frowned. Mackenzie had been strong-willed, but never sassy. Never the type to sneak into her father's store alone for an after-hours drink. Not the type to taunt him. Not the type to break the rules.

Looked like he wasn't the only one who'd changed since high school.

Don't miss
Her Homecoming Wish *by Jo McNally,*
available February 2020 wherever
Harlequin® Special Edition books and ebooks are sold.

Harlequin.com

HSEEXP0120

Get 4 FREE REWARDS!

We'll send you 2 FREE Books plus 2 FREE Mystery Gifts.

Harlequin® Special Edition books feature heroines finding the balance between their work life and personal life on the way to finding true love.

FREE
Value Over
$20

Love Harlequin romance?

DISCOVER.

Be the first to find out about promotions, news and exclusive content!

Facebook.com/HarlequinBooks

Twitter.com/HarlequinBooks

Instagram.com/HarlequinBooks

Pinterest.com/HarlequinBooks

ReaderService.com

EXPLORE.

Sign up for the Harlequin e-newsletter and download a free book from any series at **TryHarlequin.com.**

CONNECT.

Join our Harlequin community to share your thoughts and connect with other romance readers!
Facebook.com/groups/HarlequinConnection

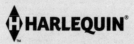

HARLEQUIN®

**ROMANCE WHEN
YOU NEED IT**

HSOCIAL2018